ECHOES
OF THE HOLLOW

C.N. NOBLE

Copyrights

Copyright © 2025 by C. N. Noble
All rights reserved.
No part of this publication may be reproduced, distributed, or transmitted in any form or by any means, including photocopying, recording, or other electronic or mechanical methods, without the prior written permission of the publisher, except as permitted by U.S. copyright law. For permission requests, contact C. N. Noble at authorc.n.noble@gmail.com.
The story, all names, characters, and incidents portrayed in this production are fictitious. No identification with actual persons (living or deceased), places, buildings, and products is intended or should be inferred.
Book Cover by GetCovers
First edition 2025

Courtesy Trigger Warnings:

This story contains scenes of emotional intensity and violence that may be upsetting to some readers. While not graphic, it includes instances of stalking, emotional manipulation, and physical confrontation. There are depictions of death and loss (both on-page and referenced), as well as supernatural possession and haunting. The narrative also touches on past trauma and familial abuse. Though the romance is closed-door and the story is low-spice, it leans heavily into gothic atmosphere, emotional intimacy, and psychological suspense.

ECHOES
OF THE HOLLOW

Also By C. N. Noble

The Orphaned King, book one in The Chronicles of Mythandria

Zeerian Creatures Field Guide: A Companion Guide to The Orphaned King

Falling for Evil, featured in the multi-author anthology, Romancing the Rogue Vol. 1

Frost & Starlight, featured in the multi-author anthology, Beyond the Depths Vol. 1: A Bite of Winter & a Sip of Trouble

Guardian of the Frostheart, a standalone novella

A Dance Of Shadows & Thorns, featured in the multi-author anthology, Romancing the Rogue Vol. 2

The Crimson Corsair, featured in the multi-author anthology, Beyond the Depths Vol. 2: Secrets of the Sea.

Dedication

In loving memory of the American artist,
Kenneth C. Madsen--my grandfather.

If not for the Norman Rockwell print of Ichabod
Crane that hung in your home, this story may have
never taken root. Thank you for passing down a love of
art, story, and imagination. Your legacy lives on.

Chapter 1
1723

"You don't understand, Silas. When I'm around her, my very soul pirouettes. It's not like any other feeling I've felt before."

"Brom will tan your hide if he hears you go on about Katrina," Silas said, his voice flat. "Third time he warns you, I won't be there to pick your teeth up."

Ichabod only grinned—an expression that made his narrow face even longer, like a delighted heron. His coat hung off his bony frame, and the breeze caught the edges of it like sails. "If you were in love with someone as intoxicatingly beautiful as Katrina Van Tassel, you'd know—there's no containing the raptures of the heart."

Silas rolled his eyes skyward with a low grunt. "I'm sure you're right."

He looked every inch the opposite of his companion—where Ichabod was long-limbed and knobby like a scarecrow, Silas was tall, yes, but lean in a way earned by labor, not lack of meals. The sleeves of his shirt clung to arms corded with quiet strength, and his hands—calloused from years of grinding grain and hauling sacks—flexed subtly at his sides, always ready to work or ward off trouble.

"I could have danced with her until morning!" Ichabod declared, plucking a violet from the edge of the footpath. "I tell you, my coming here was fated. Who would've guessed a young lady of such refinement, such elegance, would consider a humble schoolmaster for a suitor?"

"Not me. Still having trouble believing it myself."

"Not I, Silas. You really ought to come to me for more tutoring lessons. A well-turned phrase can do wonders."

"I'm a Dutch miller, Ichabod. I don't have much use for fancy words." He paused, glancing sideways, one blond curl catching in the wind before falling back just past his ear. "Flour talks louder than flattery in these parts."

The schoolmaster stooped to inhale the flower with an exaggerated sigh, his spindly legs creaking beneath him. "Mark my words, when you fall in love—truly fall in love—you'll come running for a book of sonnets."

"If I'm lucky," Silas muttered, "I'll fall for a girl who likes straight answers and strong backs."

Just then, a chill crept into the air. Fog began to snake through the trees, curling at their feet and blurring the path ahead like spilled milk in river water. Silas slowed, instinct prickling.

"Oh, Katrina—" Ichabod began again, lost in a sigh.

"Enough." Silas stopped short, his voice sharper now.

2

"Normally, I'd cheer you on, Ichabod. Heaven help me, I would. But going against Brom Bones is the kind of foolish you're not built to survive."

Ichabod blinked, adjusting his tri-cornered hat over his unruly shock of hair. "What do you mean? I did a little boxing in college—"

Silas didn't answer. His dark-blue eyes were locked on the mist, unreadable. He scanned the trees with the watchfulness of someone who'd survived more than his share of strange nights. The wind had stilled. No birds. No insects. Even the rustle of leaves seemed to hold its breath.

Fog like this's not natural, he thought grimly. Last time it rolled in this thick, old Van Ripper's dog howled till dawn—and dropped dead the next day.

"Come on," he said, jaw tight. "We need to keep moving."

Ichabod shuffled after him, flower twirling idly in his fingers and his thoughts still dancing in ballrooms, while Silas's boots sank deeper into the silence.

The path narrowed, swallowed by dew-slick vines and whispering grass. Trees arched overhead like old bones, their limbs creaking softly in the weightless air. The road from the Van Tassel estate twisted through hickory and beech, darker now—like the forest itself had begun to close in.

Ichabod, still twirling the violet between his fingers, lagged a few paces behind.

"You've got about ten more minutes to sigh over Katrina before I leave you behind," Silas called over his shoulder.

"I'm not sighing," Ichabod said, clutching the flower to his

3

chest. "I'm ruminating. It's an entirely different posture of the soul."

Silas exhaled a dry snort. "Well, ruminate faster."

The path ahead narrowed between a pair of leaning trees. A crow cawed once, somewhere high above them — then went silent. Silas adjusted the satchel on his shoulder and walked on, boots crunching over the gravel-strewn road.

"You're awfully impatient tonight," Ichabod said, catching up. "A man would think you're afraid of something."

"I'm not afraid. I'm tired."

"Of what? My love life? My charm? My striking literary wit?"

Silas shot him a look. "Of being out here after dark."

Ichabod's eyebrows lifted. "You, Washington Silas Irving, afraid of the dark? The man who once wrestled a hog in a rainstorm because it trampled your herb garden?"

"Wasn't afraid of the hog," Silas muttered. "But I've lived in these woods long enough to know what happens when you dawdle after sundown."

Ichabod tilted his head, grinning. "Are you referring to the Horseman?"

Silas gave a shrug that was more tired than dismissive. "It's an old story. Maybe it's nothing. But the ground feels different at night. And I don't like this fog."

"Come now," Ichabod said, adopting the tone of a man who had read more books than he'd lived days. "Surely, a man of reason isn't taken in by tales of phantom riders and wandering spirits. Even I know better than to let superstition get the best of me —"

"You screamed when a barn owl flew out of the rafters

last week."

"That owl came at me with murder in its eyes."

Silas let out a small laugh despite himself, but the humor faded quickly. He glanced up. The moon was barely a smear behind the thickening mist, and the branches overhead loomed like reaching fingers.

"Just … keep moving," he said. "You might not believe in ghosts, Ichabod. But the men who vanish in this wood never show up with a second opinion."

Ichabod held his chin high, lifted his arms as if framing an invisible partner, and waltzed a half step down the road.

"Like this," he said breathlessly, spinning in place. "She moved like poetry, and I — well — I matched her, step for step."

Silas didn't even look over. "You looked like you were trying to dodge bees."

"She laughed," Ichabod said, grinning. "Not mockingly, but … sweetly. As though I charmed her by accident."

"You sure it wasn't pity?"

Ichabod lowered his arms just long enough to glare at him then returned to his imaginary dance. "You're just upset because you don't appreciate the finer things — music, romance, metaphor…."

"I appreciate sleep, and we're now two miles from it."

"You'd be less bitter if you just let me teach you a few steps. Then, when you find your own Katrina, you won't stomp on her feet."

"I'm not planning on waltzing through life," Silas muttered. "I plan on working hard, getting to bed on time, and not ending up in a ditch because I poked Brom Van Brunt's pride."

Ichabod spun again, narrowly missing a low-hanging branch. "You lack vision, Silas. Romance requires risk. Besides —"

THUD.

He stopped mid-spin.

"Shush," Silas said, planting his feet.

Even the birds had gone silent.

The fog, once a thin ribbon, now rolled in heavy and low — curling around their boots, pooling at their waists, veiling the trees in pale shrouds.

Something about it felt wrong.

"Too thick for this time of year," he muttered. "Too quiet."

Then came the sound.

A low, distant thump.

Soft. Rhythmic.

Like thunder far away or a heartbeat in the earth.

Thud…

Silas straightened.

Thud-thud.

Silas's brows pulled tight. "…Did you hear that?"

His breath caught.

Just ahead, deep within the fog, something moved.

Not like a man. Not like anything natural.

He could barely make it out — only the glint of armor beneath a long, dark coat and the outline of a massive black steed. The horse snorted steam, hooves stamping the earth with a slow, deliberate rhythm. But where the rider's head should've been … there was only empty space.

And in the crook of the saddle, a sack. Burlap. Empty.

"Run," Silas whispered, but Ichabod didn't move.

So Silas shouted, louder this time. "Run, Ichabod!" he said, yanking his arm

forward with him as he too began to flee.

The path blurred beneath him, gravel scattering underfoot. His lungs burned with the chill, his heartbeat deafening. He didn't look back, trusting Ichabod would be close behind.

But the only sound behind him was his own footsteps.

No voice. No panic. No second set of feet.

Silas skidded to a stop.

"Ichabod?"

Nothing.

He turned, pushing through the suffocating fog. "Ichabod!" he shouted, louder this time. "Come on—this isn't funny!"

No answer. Only silence, thick and wrong.

A cold dread slithered through his chest and into his bones. He backtracked, each step slower, heavier—until the fog split like torn fabric.

There. The Horseman again.

He thundered past in a blur of shadow and fury, the hooves silent on the road, like a ghost given form. But this time, Silas saw it—really saw it.

The sack. The dark, crude stitching across burlap.

And the blood seeping through it.

Silas froze, the air knocked clean from his lungs. The rider vanished into the treeline, swallowed by the woods once more as he left the path silent. Cold. Empty.

Silas collapsed to his knees, as if the weight of his choices had finally crushed him.

Something near his boot caught his eye.

A single violet, flattened and torn.

His stomach twisted.

The fog pulled back, slow and unnatural, revealing the wildflowers lining the roadside — and the body crumpled among them.

Ichabod.

Silas ran, though hope was already slipping from his grasp like sand through fingers. When he reached him, the truth was undeniable.

Only blood-soaked soil remained where Ichabod's head should have been.

The Horseman had claimed another soul.

Chapter 2

Into the Hollow

(Present Day)

The rain was merciless, smearing the highway into a streak of black glass and fractured light. Evelyn gripped the steering wheel like it was the only lifeline she had left. Her knuckles, pale against the leather, had gone stiff from holding on too long.

Each mile peeled her farther away from the city — and everything she'd bled for. Her career, her credibility, the carefully structured life she'd built piece by piece … all shattered the moment her words hit the press.

She caught a glimpse of herself in the rearview mirror — hair darkened by rain and shadow, eyes rimmed with exhaustion. The high cheekbones and sharp jaw now looked gaunt, hollowed by weeks of stress. She dragged a hand through her damp dirty-blonde hair, its waves clinging to her jawline like seaweed after a storm.

The exposé on the Russo crime family had earned her the

front page. It had also earned her a death sentence.

At first, she'd brushed off the backlash as part of the job. Hate mail. Threats scribbled in shaky handwriting. Late-night voicemails that always started with her name and ended with a click.

Noise. That's all it had ever been.

Until the call.

It was a gray Thursday. Rain pattered against the newsroom windows in a steady rhythm. Evelyn stood in her glass-walled office, elbow-deep in edits, a red pen dangling from one hand as she squinted at a final paragraph.

She wore her uniform of sorts — pleated slacks, a silk blouse half-tucked from long hours, a cluster of silver rings catching the fluorescents when she moved. Her dark, dirty-blonde hair was swept into a low clip, loose strands curling around her temples from the city's humidity. Clean lines, cool polish. A look that said she belonged here. That she could bulldoze truth out of concrete if she had to.

Behind her, plaques lined the back wall — a Pulitzer finalist medallion, a framed headline from her exposé on the Westport corruption scandal, a photo of her flanked by two grim-faced senators during a congressional hearing.

The bullpen outside buzzed with low conversation and the clack of keyboards. The city hadn't slept in weeks, and neither had she.

Her desk pulsed with vibration as her cellphone began ringing. Number Unknown.

"Hello?"

"Hi, this is Detective Stanley with the NYPD. Am I speaking with Evelyn Crane?"

As she spoke, a delivery man rapped his knuckles on her office door frame.

"This is Evelyn. What can I do for you, Detective?"

She waved in the mail carrier, and stood, tucking her cell between her shoulder and cheek to sign for the delivery. Another thick envelope—likely more legal fallout. The fluorescent lights above her reflected off the faint sheen of her press badge laying atop a stack of file folders on the corner of her desk.

"Just to confirm—you're the Evelyn Crane from The Post?"

"That's me. What's going on?" she asked, scribbling her signature on the electronic pad. The carrier vanished as quickly as he had arrived.

A pause. Just long enough to knot something in her gut.

"I'm glad I caught you before you left. We've received credible intel that Vince Russo has ordered a hit on you."

Her stomach dropped. Outside, rain had just begun to fall harder, streaking the windows like ink bleeding through paper.

"I don't want you going anywhere without a police escort. Stay put. I'm en route to The Post now, and I'll follow you home myself."

Evelyn blinked, stunned. A half-laugh nearly escaped—but it stalled in her throat.

"I've had threats before, Detective. Most of them are just that. I appreciate the concern, but I think—"

"Ms. Crane," he interrupted, his tone sharp, no longer polite. "I'm not asking. I'm telling you. Stay where you are."

She tore open the envelope, a paper-cut slicing across her thumb.

"Fine. I'll meet you in the lobby."

She flipped through the documents, and her brow furrowed as the subject line caught her eye.

Estate Dowry Issued to Ms. Evelyn Crane.

That had been four hours ago.

When Evelyn and Detective Stanley made it to her flat, her front door frame was badly damaged, and her entire place ransacked. Not in the way that said someone was looking for something. No, this was personal. It felt hostile. The detective stayed with Evelyn while she quickly packed a couple of bags. Oddly, until she received the envelope with the deed to a mysterious ancestral home, she didn't have anywhere else she could go. Now she had a cottage in some tiny town called Sleepy Hollow. In her ten years of investigative journalism, she hadn't ever heard of it before, so she was surprised to find out it was within driving distance from the city.

The good detective followed her to the edge of the city as promised before turning back. Assuming he did his job well, no one would know where she was or where she was heading. She glanced into the rearview mirror again. A habit now. Always checking. Always watching.

If she was being followed, it would be near impossible to tell with the monsoon of water falling from the sky. The rhythmic slap of the wipers didn't help her anxiety either. She had watched too many thriller films to miss the cliches in her current situation. On the run. Rainy. Alone. Heading toward a town she didn't even know existed until a few hours ago. Even the timing of receiving the deed to the property was suspicious.

In her ten-minute web search about the town, she learned Sleepy Hollow was secluded. Quiet. And now she had a deed to an old family property there, passed to her after the death of an estranged relative she'd never met or heard of. The lawyer's letter had been vague. Too vague. But Evelyn didn't have time to be picky.

She winced as a flash of lightning split the sky. Her nerves were shot, strung tight and buzzing. Every road sign that flew past made her stomach clench.

SLEEPY HOLLOW – 6 MILES

Almost there.

Her phone buzzed once and went dark.

No signal.

Figures.

She lowered it with a sigh, eyes drifting back to the road just as a blaring horn sounded. A blinding flood of headlights burst through the downpour — blazing. She was in the wrong lane.

Her heart lurched into her throat.

She yanked the wheel.

POP.

The sound snapped like a gunshot.

Her car lurched, skidding sideways in a scream of tires and water.

Rain sheeted across the windshield. Her world twisted — sky, trees, road all spinning.

Then — impact.

Metal groaned.

The car crashed nose-first into the ditch, the front end slamming into the mud like a fist into wet clay.

The back wheels lifted then thudded back down, crooked and half-buried.

Everything stilled.

She was tilted forward, pressed into her seatbelt, breath shallow and fast. Her hair clung to her face in damp strands. Cold mud spattered the cracked window beside her.

She gripped the wheel like it was the only solid thing left. Her chest rose and fell in sharp bursts. The only sound was the relentless drumming of rain on the roof, a punishing rhythm that drowned out thought.

Something stung.

She looked down. A thin red line curved across the top of her hand, blood beading up before it trickled down her arm. The windshield was broken and rain water was trickling in.

Still breathing. Still conscious.

Just scraped. Shaken. Alive.

The dash lights flickered once and died.

She fumbled for her phone again, hoping maybe — just maybe — but the screen was black. One blinking battery icon. No bars. No rescue.

Then — lights.

Blue and red flashed across the trees like an eerie pulse.

A cruiser. Just across the road, its strobes painted the storm in bursts of color.

14

A car door creaked open.

She could just make out the silhouette of a man stepping into the deluge, his shape carved in lightning — broad-shouldered, calm, purposeful.

Water splashed under heavy boots as he crossed the highway. A flashlight bobbed in his hand, cutting through the rain like a blade.

He approached the slanted car and rapped gently on the glass.

"Evening, ma'am," he said, his voice muffled by rain but smooth and steady. "You alright in there?"

She blinked, breath caught in her throat. Her gaze flicked to the insignia on his coat —

Sleepy Hollow Sheriff's Department.

Her fingers clenched the wheel again. She'd made it. Sleepy Hollow.

"Yeah," she called out breathlessly. "I think so."

The officer tried pulling on the door handle, but it was locked.

Evelyn tried the electronic unlock button but got no response. She manually pulled the lock up, and the officer carefully opened the door.

"I'm Officer Downey from Bridge County Police."

"I appreciate you stopping, Officer Downey. I'm Evelyn."

"Do you think you can move alright?" he asked.

She nodded. "Yeah. I believe so. I'm just a little shook up is all."

He glanced at her bloodied hand as she swept her hair away from her eyes.

"You're hurt," he said, gesturing to her wound. "I can call a paramedic — "

"Oh, yeah. It's not that bad, actually," she quickly interrupted. "I will be alright."

The last thing she wanted was for anyone to know where she was, and anybody could be listening to police scanners for her whereabouts.

"Just ... lost control."

He opened the door, offering a gloved hand. "Let's get you somewhere inside. You're lucky. Not many folks come out this way anymore."

Evelyn hesitated then slid her hand into his.

"I'm not here by accident," she murmured, more to herself than to him.

He pulled her out of the car and made sure she was steady on her feet before tilting his head with curiosity. "No?"

"I read something on the internet about the town and got curious. Thought I'd take a break from city life for a minute."

The lie was easy. Practiced.

But something flickered in the sheriff's eyes. A flicker of recognition — or suspicion.

"I'll call a tow in the morning for you."

"Thank you. I appreciate that."

"Do you need anything from your car before we leave?"

"Um, yeah," she thought. Carefully, she reached in and pulled a lever on the middle console and the trunk popped. She grabbed her jacket and purse as she came back out. "I have a couple bags in the trunk."

"I can grab those for you. Stand up on the side of the road away from the car. It will be safer there."

"Thank you." She stepped away, but her suspicious nature wouldn't allow her to take her eyes off of him while he was near her car.

The officer didn't linger. He took hold of the two leather bags and closed the trunk before taking calculated steps up the muddy hill to the road.

Thunder grumbled overhead, low and long, as the rain came down in sheets. It drowned out every other sound.

"Let's get you in the car," Officer Downey called, already jogging toward his cruiser.

Evelyn followed, water sloshing in her boots, hair plastered to her face.

Once she was settled in the back seat, she took quick stock of herself. Soaked to the bone. Bruised, scraped, but in one piece. She peered through the window at her car, half-submerged in the ditch, nose down.

Stupid. So stupid.

The hatch of the cruiser thumped shut, and Officer Downey climbed in, rain dripping from his hat and shoulders.

"Whew!" he said, swiping water from his face. "Haven't seen rain like this in a while. You must've brought it with you."

Evelyn gave a tired smile and leaned toward the glass. "Is there a hotel nearby?"

"There's an inn. Not far."

"Would you mind taking me there?"

He started the engine. "Wouldn't be doing my job if I didn't."

17

"Thanks," she said, voice quiet.

Outside, lightning split the sky in half.

Chapter 3

A Van Tassel Welcome

A few miles down the highway, the cruiser slowed to a stop at a four-way intersection. Officer Downey paused long enough to make it textbook then turned right onto a narrower road framed by towering trees. Their limbs tangled high overhead, forming a tunnel that swallowed the headlights more and more with every mile.

A white sign glared in the dark as they passed, its freshly painted letters illuminated by the cruiser's beams: Welcome to Sleepy Hollow.

No houses. No storefronts. Not even a gas station. Just the rain and the trees pressing in like curious onlookers.

"Where did the town go?" Evelyn asked, a teasing lilt in her voice.

In the rearview mirror, she caught the flicker of Downey's glance. "It's just around the bend," he said. "Not far."

The windshield wipers strained at full speed, slapping

rhythmically against glass that blurred faster than it cleared.

Downey reached for the heat controls and clicked them on. Warm air began to push through the vents. He peeled off his soaked hat and set it in the passenger seat.

"Sure is comin' down," he muttered, thunder cracking faintly in the distance.

As they rounded a wide curve, lights bloomed in the fog ahead — soft, scattered pinpricks across broad swaths of land. Porch lights. Barn lamps. Yard posts. It was like the town had decided not to gather in one place but stretch its limbs over acres.

They rounded a curve, and lights started to appear. Dim porch bulbs. Security lights on outbuildings. A few windows lit up in the distance. The homes were spaced far apart, each tucked into its own patch of land.

Then came a small row of buildings near the road, closer together — probably the center of town. A flashing yellow light signaled the turnoff ahead. It was quiet. No other cars. No pedestrians.

The fog thickened as they approached, curling low across the road and blurring the edges of everything. Lights ahead glowed soft and hazy through the mist.

Evelyn leaned closer to the window, watching as Sleepy Hollow came into view — quiet, shuttered, still.

Every storefront was dark.

Evelyn glanced at her watch and pressed the side button to light the face.

7:12 p.m.

"Does Sleepy Hollow always shut down this early?" she

asked, lifting a brow.

"Yep," Officer Downey replied without missing a beat. "Used to be everything closed by five. Town meeting changed that — gave folks an extra couple hours to grab what they need after work."

He shrugged, eyes fixed on the road ahead.

"Not that it made much difference. Old habits die hard."

"I can't decide if that's charming or a little creepy."

He chuckled. "That's about what most newcomers say. Give it a day or two — it grows on you. Or it won't."

They reached a roundabout with a tall, weather-worn statue at its center. Its features were swallowed by shadow, distorted by the gathering mist.

Moments later, Officer Downey pulled up in front of a grand two-story brick building. A lamplight above the door flickered, casting a soft glow on the polished plaque near the steps.

Van Tassel Inn.

He stepped out and rounded the car. As Evelyn opened her door, he shut it behind her with a firm click.

"Well," he said, pausing beside her. "Welcome to Sleepy Hollow, Ms. ...?"

She offered a polite smile, ignoring the bait. "Thank you, Officer. I appreciate the ride."

His eyes lingered a moment too long, curious but not unkind. "Sure thing," he said, the words drawn out like a question he'd decided not to ask.

"I'll get your bags," he added, moving toward the trunk.

She stood by the curb, hands tucked into her coat pockets,

pretending not to notice his sideways glance. The silence stretched as he handed over her bags.

"If you need anything, the station's just down the road," he said, his tone casual — almost too casual.

"I'll keep that in mind," she replied. "Goodnight, Officer Downey."

He hesitated then tipped his hat. "Night, ma'am."

She watched his taillights disappear around the bend before turning toward the inn, heart tapping a little faster than before.

The bell above the inn's door jingled weakly as Evelyn stepped inside, soaked to the bone and gripping her bags like they were the last solid thing in the world. The warmth inside hit her like a breath of comfort — wood-paneled walls, the scent of old books and cinnamon, and the gentle crackle of a fire at the far end of a sitting room off to the left.

At the front desk, no one stood behind the small brass bell. Evelyn tapped it once, then again, before deciding to wait.

To her right, in a cozy seating area near the hearth, four older men played cards and sipped steaming mugs of something that smelled like mulled cider and whiskey. Their conversation, low and gravelly, floated over in between card slaps and bursts of laughter.

"…say what you will, but it always starts with the fog."

"Oh, hush now, no need to scare the tourists before they've even got a room key," one said, casting a glance her way.

Evelyn offered a polite smile and folded her arms. She wasn't trying to eavesdrop — well, maybe a little.

"That's alright. I don't scare easy."

The men exchanged knowing glances, not really hiding their obvious amusement.

"That's always how the story starts for some reason," the old one said.

"How what starts?" Evelyn asked, genuinely curious.

"Why, the stories of the Headless Horseman, of course," another replied in an ominous tone. "Haven't you heard the old Sleepy Hollow legend?"

They chuckled among themselves, not unkindly.

"I'd never even heard of this place until today." She took a chair from a nearby table and sat with them. "Who is this Headless Horseman?"

"Some say he was a bloodthirsty Hessian soldier," the tallest one replied, his voice a rumble. "Lost his head to a cannonball during the war. Now he rides again, especially come autumn. Cold nights. Fog in the trees. Looking for what he's lost."

"But," another voiced in, "locals know better than to believe in such fantastic ideas. The real monsters are nothing more than flesh and bone."

The third elderly gentleman leaned over the table. "Either way, if you're not careful, you'll end up just like Ichabod. Or one of the other poor souls still wandering this town."

"Who?" Evelyn tilted her head, suppressing a half-smile at the name.

"Ichabod Crane."

Evelyn's smile faltered when she heard the last name.

"Schoolmaster. Real superstitious type." The man leaned back in his chair, his mug cradled in both hands like a storyteller preparing a ghost tale. "Came here a long time ago. Courting a local girl, poking his nose where it didn't belong."

"What happened to him?" she asked, tone lighter than she felt.

"Disappeared," said the first man. "Fog rolled in, thick as smoke. He and his friend were heading home from the Van Tassel home. Only one of them escaped the Horseman's blade."

"Ichabod?"

The men exchanged glances.

"No. Unfortunately, his body was found along the road that runs through the woods," said the one closest to the fire. "Not his head though. Just the rest of him."

"And his friend?" Evelyn asked softly, heart thudding.

"Silas?"

A shrug. A sip of cider. Silence.

"Never seen again. Some say the Hessian returned for him later that night. Others believe the pain of his betrayal was too much to bear and he took his own life."

Evelyn swallowed hard. She wasn't one for superstitions, but she paid attention when someone spoke with conviction— when belief settled into their voice like something remembered, not imagined.

"What are you relics going on about now?" a voice from just behind her shoulder questioned.

Evelyn nearly jumped out of her seat.

"Mind your business, Peter," one of the old men grumbled with a smirk.

Evelyn turned toward the voice and found a man standing just off to her side—young, well-kept, dressed in dark jeans and a fitted button-up rolled at the sleeves. He had that polished, small-town charm that felt almost practiced, like someone who knew exactly what kind of impression he left in a room.

"These ancient ruins aren't boring you with one of their far-fetched horror stories, are they, Ms. ...?"

Evelyn half-smiled, glancing at each of the men. "Not at all. I love a good story." She stood from her seat and held out her hand to him. "Evelyn."

He clasped it gently—calloused fingers, steady grip, just enough pressure to seem confident without overdoing it.

"Evelyn," he echoed, and his smile flickered wider, revealing a dimple on one side. The kind of smile that probably worked better than truth in a town like this.

"Welcome to Sleepy Hollow. I'm Peter Van Tassel. Will you be staying the night with us?"

"I was hoping to. Do you have a room available?"

"I certainly do. If you've had your fill of the scent of decay," he said, gesturing to the old men, "I can get you squared away."

"Funny," one of the men replied before sipping his coffee.

Another leaned back in his chair with a low chuckle. "Careful, Peter. Stories like that run in your blood."

Peter paused mid-step, his grin still in place—but just a little tighter now. Evelyn caught the flicker of tension.

"Then it's a good thing I know how to keep them in check."

"Thank you, yes. I am pretty tired," Evelyn said quickly, offering him an easy exit.

"Well, alright then. Right this way."

She followed him to the front desk, her worn leather bags

piled beside it. Up close, she took in the neat fade of his light-brown hair—short on the sides, a few inches longer on top, styled with clean precision. His posture was easy, but there was intention behind it. Toned arms beneath rolled sleeves, five o'clock shadow trimmed just enough to look effortless. Cute, sure—but not dangerously so. Comfortable in his skin.

Not that she was analyzing him. Not really. Descriptors came second nature after years in journalism—file it, frame it, move on. A force of habit more than interest. Or so she told herself while denying herself the moment to just enjoy the view.

"That all you brought with you?" he asked, eyeing her bags as he stepped behind the counter.

"Yeah. I'm just here for a short time."

"Oh? For work? Or …" His voice trailed off, letting the question linger.

"Yeah," she said, flashing a polite smile that didn't invite more.

Peter paused, clearly hoping she'd elaborate.

She didn't. Not because she was unaware—just not in the habit of offering strangers her life story.

He turned to the computer, fingers tapping softly at the keys. "You from the city?"

She hesitated. "Yeah. I mean … I've lived a few places, but most recently, a city."

He nodded. But she caught the flicker of interest—mild but unmistakable.

To smooth the moment, she added, "What about you? Have you always lived here?"

"Oh yeah. Born and raised. The Van Tassel line goes way

back in these parts."

She nodded. "Must be nice."

"As a teenager, I dreamed about getting out. And I did — for a while," he said, eyes still on the screen. "But then my grandparents passed. Just a month apart from one another."

"Oh." Her voice softened. "I'm sorry."

"Thanks. It's been a few years now. I've had time to" — he gave a small smile — "adjust. They raised me since I was little. So when I inherited this place, it felt like … the last real connection I had left."

There was something steady about the way he said it. Anchored. He didn't seem like the kind of man who ran from ghosts.

Connection, Evelyn thought. It was something she hadn't felt in a long time.

"I think it's great you decided to stay and keep this place going," she said, a smile tugging at the corner of her mouth. "Especially tonight."

Peter chuckled. "Right — back to checking you in. Can I get your last name, Evelyn?"

She blinked.

A last name.

"Cooper," she said quickly, borrowing her editor's.

"Alright. And will you be paying with a card? We just went high-tech last week." He tapped the shiny new reader with mock pride.

Evelyn smiled. "Nice. But no — I've got cash."

Always carry cash. One of the first things she'd learned in the field.

"How much for the night?"

"Forty-five dollars," Peter said, visibly proud.

Evelyn blinked. That was it?

She glanced around. Warm, clean, well-kept. Honestly, she'd expected at least double.

But she wasn't about to complain.

She pulled exact change from her wallet. "Forty-five, it is."

"Thank you," he said, sliding the bills into the till.

"If you think you'll be around tomorrow," he said as he turned toward the key rack, "there are a few historical sites I can show you. Local favorites."

He handed her a brass key with a number 6 centered at eye level.

"Thanks. I've got a few things to do first, but I might have time afterward...."

"Perfect! I'll meet you at the coffee shop down the street. Twelve o'clock work?"

"Yeah, okay," she said, grabbing her bags.

Peter moved quickly around the counter. "Allow me."

"Oh, I've got it."

"Please?" he said, already reaching.

Evelyn arched a brow. "Are you out to win a chivalry award or something?"

His crooked grin deepened, that dimple flickering again. "Actually, I'm procrastinating folding towels."

She chuckled. "Ah, the truth comes out."

"I appreciate you indulging me."

Peter hoisted the bags easily over his shoulder and led the

way up the stairs.

"Room six is on the left. Quieter, overlooks the back garden."

"Sounds nice."

At the top of the landing, he unlocked the door and stepped aside. The scent of lavender and cedar greeted her. Warm golden light filtered through the curtains, softening the room's edges.

Peter set her bags just inside.

"If you need anything, there's a phone on the nightstand. Dial zero, and I'll come running—unless the towels have claimed me."

Evelyn smiled. "I'll keep that in mind."

They lingered in the doorway a moment longer than necessary.

"Well," Peter said, backing away, "twelve o'clock. Coffee shop."

"I'll be there," she said, though even as the words left her mouth, her thoughts were already drifting toward the secrets waiting for her at her new parcel of property.

As the door clicked shut behind him, Evelyn exhaled slowly and turned toward the window.

Rain drizzled down the moonlit glass. Below, the garden glowed with scattered lanterns and the soft haze of patio lights strung over empty garden tables. A thin fog had begun to creep in.

Evelyn drew the curtain closed and began removing her jewelry, setting each ring and bracelet on the nightstand with a quiet clink. Her thoughts were frayed at the edges, pulling in too many directions. A death threat on her name. A family estate she'd never heard of. A car wrecked in a ditch. And now ...

stories of headless specters riding through town like something straight from a fever dream.

It was a lot.

She reached into her bag and pulled out the deed, her thumb brushing the edge of the yellowed paper. Crane Cottage. The name was printed in elegant script, but it felt more like a warning than a welcome. It still didn't make sense — why it had come when it did, why it had come to her. A deed to a family estate she had never heard about, just as the walls in New York were closing in. As if Sleepy Hollow had been waiting.

She let the page fall back into her bag and exhaled. Small town life wasn't something she had ever pictured for herself. She wasn't used to the quiet or how time seemed to slow down in rural places. Then again, she hadn't stayed anywhere long enough to find out if that was a bad thing or good. Maybe Peter was just a charming detour. A well-timed distraction to get her through her short time here.

Whether or not that was a good thing was still to be determined.

Chapter 4
Lineage & Lies

T he storm had passed by morning, but Sleepy Hollow still clung to the scent of wet earth and woodsmoke. Clouds hung low over the hills like a second ceiling, and fog curled through the trees like it had nowhere else to be.

Evelyn left the Van Tassel Inn just after seven, stepping into the mist with her collar turned up and her nerves tightly wound. Her first stop was the small real estate office on the edge of the town square—Hudson Valley Property & Deeds etched in peeling gold letters on the window. Inside, it smelled faintly of old paper and lemon cleaner.

The woman behind the desk looked up from her computer with a bright but professional smile. "Morning. You must be Ms. Crane."

Evelyn stiffened at the name then stepped forward with a carefully measured smile. "Yes. But—please. I'd prefer that not be repeated around town. I'm just here to finalize the paperwork."

The woman blinked then nodded, her smile faltering just slightly. "Of course. Discretion is part of the job. I'm Carla."

"Thank you, Carla. I appreciate it."

Carla smiled as she led the way. "Well, it's not every day we get someone new tied to a legacy like yours. Between the Cranes and the Van Tassels, this town has more ghost stories than streetlights."

"Sounds like I'm walking into a campfire tale," she said with a small laugh.

But Carla's words stuck like a thorn. Cranes and Van Tassels. The way she said it, like a pairing carved in the foundation of this place — whether Evelyn wanted a part of it or not.

"Don't let it get to ya. They are just tales, after all," she reassured. "Right this way. I've already drawn up the transfer documents. Just a few signatures and it'll be official."

Evelyn followed her into the narrow room, noting the framed photos of local properties and a certificate of licensure on the wall. A folder lay open on the desk, pages neatly arranged with yellow signature tabs.

As Evelyn skimmed the top sheet, she asked, "Does the deed list the previous owner? I didn't recognize the name on the letter I received."

"Let's see…" Carla flipped a few pages forward, her finger trailing down a column. "Yes — listed here as Barnaby Crane."

Her grandfather.

They'd had little connection. Her mother had kept Evelyn's father's side of the family at arm's length ever since his death — an unspoken boundary Evelyn had never dared cross.

Questions had always been met with tight-lipped answers or outright deflection. He died when she was young, too young to remember his face. All she had were fragments, passed through vague comments or overheard conversations.

But if Evelyn had to guess, it all came down to inheritance. Or bitterness. Or both.

"Looks like he passed about six months ago. He'd been the legal owner for quite some time. The property came to him through a trust." Carla slid the paperwork across the desk. "If you'll just sign where the yellow tabs are, you'll be all set," she said, offering a pen.

Evelyn took the seat across from her and accepted it, fingers tightening slightly around the barrel. She hovered for a moment then bent to sign.

Evelyn Crane.

Her signature flowed smoothly—elegant, sharp. The kind of penmanship born from years of signing off on high-stakes documents under pressure. But as the ink settled into the page, a prickle crept up the back of her neck.

Something shifted. Small. Palpable. Like she'd just signed a blood oath, and the universe had taken note.

She blinked, easing back in the chair behind her, unsettled.

"Do you have anything that says how long the house has been in the family? Or who lived there before him?"

Carla gave a polite shrug. "Not in this packet. The deed confirms ownership, but if you're looking for deeper history— property lines, previous occupants—that kind of detail would be down in the courthouse archives. Everything before digital went into the basement."

"Basement," Evelyn echoed, almost under her breath. "Of course they do."

"If you're looking for more background on the house — or the Crane family line — you might find something there. Gregory keeps everything well organized. He's the clerk. That man really knows his way around the archives."

Evelyn signed the last page with a firm stroke. "I'll check it out. Thank you for pointing me in the right direction."

Carla handed her a single brass key on a simple ring. "Here you go. It's yours now. I'd recommend keeping the porch light on at night. Folks around here say it helps with the fog."

Evelyn paused at the door, glancing back. "Is that just town superstition? Or does the fog get that bad?"

Carla gave a smile that didn't quite reach her eyes. "Depends on who you ask."

Evelyn nodded once and slipped the key into her coat pocket. "Well … I'll see for myself, I suppose. Thanks again, Carla."

"Any time."

It was nine-thirty by the time Evelyn made her way to the courthouse. A squat brick building with ivy crawling up its sides, it looked older than the town around it, as though it had been dropped into Sleepy Hollow from a previous century. She stepped inside, the scent of mildew and old books clinging to the air.

She followed the signs to the basement, where dim fluorescent lights buzzed faintly and the linoleum floor squeaked beneath her boots. At the end of the hall sat a single desk, cluttered with yellowing papers and a half-finished cup of coffee. Behind it, a balding man in his sixties worked at a crossword puzzle.

"Local records?" he asked without looking up.

"Property lines," Evelyn said. "For the Crane residence."

That got his attention. He looked up, squinting at her over his glasses. "You mean the Crane place? The cottage out on Hollow Road?"

"That's the one. I'm the new owner."

He let out a low whistle and stood, stretching with a slight grunt. "Didn't think anyone would ever live there again. Follow me."

"Well, didn't the previous owner live there?"

"The previous six owners have chosen not to inhabit that house. At least, not for long."

Evelyn stopped mid-step.

"Six?" she repeated.

He didn't answer—just continued down the narrow row of filing cabinets, one hand trailing the spines as he moved.

Evelyn followed, slower now, her thoughts already racing. Six owners. And none of them stayed.

Why?

Inheritance drama? Family feuds? Or something else entirely?

The area was rows and stacks of dust and secrets layered together like sediment.

She tucked a loose strand of hair behind her ear, unease prickling beneath her skin.

He pulled open a drawer with a groan of rusted metal.

"Should be here somewhere…"

Evelyn tried to steady her breath, but her pulse didn't listen. For the first time since signing that deed, she felt less like she was claiming a family legacy — and more like she was stepping into a vacancy that no one had dared to fill.

"We don't get many people down here," he said. "Town's old, but the folks tend to forget that. Records go way back though — Crane, Van Tassel, Van Brunt … names you see more in ghost stories than in tax ledgers."

"Well, I'm a little interested in both," Evelyn replied, crouching beside him as he laid out a stack of manila folders. "Do these show property boundaries too?"

"Yep. Deeds, surveys, transfer records — some of it's a mess. I'll warn you, it might take a while to make sense of it."

Gregory carried the stack of folders around the corner to an area with a couple of open tables, a copy machine, and a row of old computers.

"Each folder is labeled according to contents. I only keep facts in the archive. If you're looking for lore or folk tales, you'll have to google it or ask someone in town."

"I appreciate it. Thank you for your help."

"It will take you some time to get through all of this. You're welcome to bring food in if you'd like, just make sure to keep it on a separate surface, so the records don't get ruined from spills," he asked.

"Thanks. I will."

Evelyn leafed through a few documents, scanning the hand-written notations. Names, surveyor stamps, boundary descriptions—all archaic, many written in longhand script that required patience to decode. She flipped between pages, cross-referencing them like puzzle pieces.

Crane. Van Tassel. Van Brunt.

A pattern was beginning to form. It wasn't just one property—multiple parcels had passed between these families for centuries, some split and reunited through marriage or inheritance. Some of the notations were in Latin. Others bore initials she didn't recognize. She jotted notes in her leather-bound planner, underlining references that might point to other heirs or land tied to the estate.

She pulled one map closer, tracing the property lines with her finger. The land surrounding the cottage had shrunk over time—absorbed, repurposed, renamed—but there was something odd about the way it wrapped around the treeline. A border that didn't conform to any natural feature. She frowned, flipping to the back of the file for more recent notes.

Gregory's earlier words echoed in her mind—ghost stories and tax ledgers. Maybe the truth lived somewhere between.

She checked her watch and nearly cursed.

"Gregory?" she called, poking her head around the corner. "Would it be possible to get copies of all of this? Everything tied to the Crane property line and ownership records? I'm running short on time, but I want to look through it all more carefully."

Gregory scratched the back of his neck. "Sure, but it ain't fast. Our copier's from the Stone Age."

She smiled faintly. "That's fine. I've got somewhere to be, but I can come back later."

He gave a short nod and walked over to the copier to turn it on. "Give me a couple hours. I'll have a stack waiting."

Evelyn hesitated before turning away. "Have you ever been out there? To the Crane place?"

"Once. Years ago. My father sent me to pick up a box of old books when I was a kid. Didn't stay long. Place gave me the creeps. Still does."

"Because of the stories? Or something else?"

Gregory shrugged. "Maybe both. But the fog gets real thick out that way. And no one ever sees it coming. It's eerie." He shrugged. "Enough to keep me away."

Evelyn nodded slowly, her fingers brushing over the edge of one of the old maps. "Thanks, Gregory. I'll be back this afternoon."

"I'll be here," he said, already hunched over the copier. "Watch your step on the stairs. They're slick when it's damp."

She offered a grateful smile then turned and hurried down the hall. Time was slipping away.

The coffee shop was only a block away, tucked between a gift boutique and a bakery. It smelled of cinnamon and espresso when she pushed through the door, hair damp from the fog. Her eyes scanned the small seating area.

Peter was already there, seated at a corner table with two steaming ready-to-go cups. He glanced up as she entered and raised a brow with a playful smirk, standing when he saw her. "I was about to send out a search party."

She smiled, breathless. "Sorry — I got caught up in courthouse paperwork. You didn't wait long, did you?"

He handed her a cup. "Long enough to know the cinnamon rolls here are dangerous."

"Oo, sounds tempting," she said cupping her hands around the paper collar around her cup.

"Have you eaten yet?"

"Not yet. I'm starved." Evelyn lifted the cup to her nose, inhaling slowly, curious. The scent was sweet — warm cinnamon, pumpkin, and a whisper of caramel. Definitely not her usual.

She'd always preferred her coffee black. Direct. Undistracted. A reflection of her life: sharp edges, no room for indulgence. This was the opposite — soft, spiced, almost comforting.

"Let me grab you something you can eat on the go, then."

"On the go? You're anxious to get started," she teased.

"There's lots to show you. I'll be right back."

She watched him head to the counter, quietly surprised he hadn't asked what she liked. But if he was paying, she wasn't going to complain.

Evelyn took a cautious sip. The temperature was perfect — warm and smooth, the rich espresso mellowed by sweet pumpkin and spice. A pumpkin caramel latte, she realized, with just enough cinnamon and nutmeg to linger on her tongue.

Comfort in a cup. Thoughtful, too.

She liked it.

For a moment, she let herself relax. The warmth of the coffee in her hands, the casual way Peter spoke to her, the inviting hum of conversation around them — it all chipped away at the walls she'd carefully kept up. Still, a whisper of caution stirred at the back of her mind. People here smiled easily, but so far, everyone seemed to know more than they let on.

A moment later, Peter returned with a small brown bag. "Here," he said, handing it to her. "House specialty. We call it a Sleepy Hollow Rider. Roast turkey, sharp cheddar, apple butter, and arugula on warm sourdough. Easy to eat while walking. Locals swear it wards off ghosts."

Evelyn peeked inside and smiled. "This looks amazing."

"It tastes even better than it looks. Now, come with me. There is much to see, and half of the day is already gone."

She laughed, getting to her feet. "Lead the way. Just don't let me get lost in the fog."

Peter offered a warm grin, but there was something tight behind it — like a string pulled just a little too taut.

"Stick with me. I know all the shortcuts."

Chapter 5
Unpacking Secrets

The midday sky had cleared by the time they stepped back out into the street, the sunshine brightening the brick façades and warming the pavement underfoot. Evelyn balanced her coffee in one hand and the warm brown bag in the other as Peter led the way.

"Okay, tour guide," she said, raising an eyebrow. "Where to first?"

Peter gestured toward the roundabout at the edge of town. "I figured we'd start with what everyone sees when they first arrive in Sleepy Hollow."

They made their way to the circular green, where the fog had finally lifted enough to reveal the full figure. A life-sized statue of a man on horseback loomed at the center, a pumpkin on his shoulders and his head tucked under one arm.

"Is that …?" Evelyn trailed off, tilting her head.

"Yep," Peter said. "The Headless Horseman in all his

bronze glory."

Evelyn let out a quiet laugh. "Subtle."

Peter grinned. "Sleepy Hollow doesn't do subtle. We embrace our legacy—ghosts and all."

She stepped closer, taking in the fine details—the wild motion of the horse, the way the cape billowed around the rider. "Honestly? It's kind of impressive."

Peter walked a slow circle around the base of the statue, hands tucked in his jacket pockets. "Legend says he rides through town when the fog's thickest, looking for what he lost."

"His head?"

Peter leaned in like he was about to tell her a secret. "Or something more important. That part depends on who you ask."

He said it with a grin, but something about the way he looked at her—really looked at her—sent a flicker of unease down her spine. It passed quickly, drowned in another joke.

She let it go. He was probably just trying to be playful.

Evelyn smirked. "Cryptic. I like it."

From there, they wandered down narrow cobblestone streets. Peter pointed out century-old buildings and shared short, occasionally embellished stories about each. He held doors open, steered her around muddy puddles, and slowed his pace when hers did.

"That old house there," he said, nodding toward a two-story colonial with black shutters, "was once a stop on the Underground Railroad."

"Seriously?"

He nodded. "Town's small, but its history is bigger than

most people expect."

They passed the old schoolhouse next. Evelyn paused at the wrought-iron gate.

"Is this …?"

Peter smiled. "Where Ichabod Crane taught. Or so the legend claims."

"Interesting. What does local lore say about Ichabod Crane?" she asked, eyeing the crooked bell tower.

"Well, nothing overly impressive."

"Oh? Was he a scoundrel?" she asked teasingly.

"No, nothing like that. From what I understand, he was book smart, but that's about it. He was tall, skinny, awkward, and probably more conceited than he had right to be."

"Ouch," she said with a look of pity. "Poor guy."

"Eh, don't pity him too much. Apparently, there was enough about him that he caught the eye of the prettiest young woman in town."

"Is that right?"

"It is. Ms. Katrina Van Tassel wrote in her journal that she and Ichabod were becoming quite the item."

"Wow. Your ancestor, huh?"

"Yep. Though, it's still uncertain if she was trying to make her previous beau, Brom, jealous." He shrugged. "I guess we'll never know. The night she had written that was the night Ichabod had met the Horseman on the road."

"Oh! Geez."

Peter turned toward her, his voice softer. "You really didn't know about any of this before coming here?"

"Nope. It's all news to me."

He gave a thoughtful nod, motioning down a shaded path lined with ancient oak trees. "Cemetery's that way. If you're brave."

"I think I've met my legend quota for the day," Evelyn replied, nudging him with her elbow.

Peter grinned. "Fair enough. I don't go there much myself. Never liked how quiet it gets," he said with a chuckle that didn't quite ring true. "One last stop, then."

They made their way back toward the Van Tassel Inn as the sun dipped behind the clouds. Peter held the door open, and they stepped into the warmth of the lobby.

"Before I let you collapse from all the history, there's one last thing I want to show you."

He led her to the far end of the hallway, where a framed collection of old photographs and documents lined the wall.

"This," he said, gesturing to the display, "is my family's legacy. The Van Tassels. Been running the inn for generations."

Evelyn stepped closer, reading the names and dates etched into brass plaques. "This one's from 1785," she murmured. "Peter Van Tassel the first?"

Peter nodded. "My namesake. And if the stories are true, he was Katrina's younger brother."

She glanced sideways at him, a smile tugging at her lips. "Who did she end up marrying?"

He shrugged, a mischievous glint in his eyes. "Her childhood friend and former suitor. Abraham Van Brunt, or 'Brom Bones', as they called him."

"Interesting."

"What is?"

"Well, you have a jealous ex lover, a murderous ghost, and a vulnerable young lady who stands to inherit a sizable estate.... Just makes one wonder if there was something more sinister at play than a ghost."

"I'm not sure I understand what you're implying. Are you suggesting Brom might have been responsible for Ichabod's demise?"

Evelyn shrugged. "Who am I to know? I just arrived in Sleepy Hollow. It does make me curious, though."

Peter gazed at the wall filled with lineage before them. "The Van Tassels did have a way of surviving. When others didn't."

They stood there in the hush of the hallway, the past staring down at them through yellowed frames.

"Thanks for the tour," Evelyn said, finally breaking the silence. "Really."

Peter dipped his head. "Anytime. There's more of Sleepy Hollow to see … but that'll have to wait." He paused. "Will you be staying here another night, or—?"

"Actually, I'll be checking out. Just need to gather my things."

"Oh? Somewhere close by?"

"Just outside the village. But you'll see me around," she added with a small smile.

Peter nodded. "Good. I'll get you squared away up front, then."

"Thanks. I appreciate that."

He stepped back, leaving her alone with the wall of names. Evelyn studied the faces, the quiet smiles frozen in time. The Van Tassel name had endured a lot of speculation and trauma.

And Peter —

Evelyn glanced over her shoulder just as he vanished around the corner.

Maybe he was just proud of his roots. It made sense. Still, something about the way he talked about legacy ... like it wasn't just history. Like it was something still being played out.

And now ... she knew more of hers.

Yet no one but Carla knew it.

Not Peter. Not Gregory.

She hadn't lied — just kept the most dangerous truths close to the chest. If the Russo family had somehow traced her this far, one slip of the tongue could undo everything. For now, she was simply Evelyn, the woman who inherited a house she barely understood.

Still, staring at those old names and sepia-toned faces, something inside her stirred. Legacy. Belonging. And the quiet, nagging sense that she was meant to be here for reasons deeper than she could admit.

Even to herself.

Her gaze returned to the framed pieces on the wall — newspaper clippings, aging documents, brittle certificates — but it was the painting in the center that held her.

It was a harvest scene, rich in autumn tones. A group posed in front of what appeared to be the old Van Tassel estate, surrounded by golden fields and the crisp suggestion of falling leaves. The style was traditional, slightly romanticized — the faces just detailed enough to suggest real people, though softened by time and brushstroke.

At the bottom of the gilded frame, a brass plate read:

"Van Tassel Harvest Gathering – Autumn, 1723"

Evelyn stepped closer.

Toward the right stood a tall man with a narrow frame, his posture slightly awkward, a small bouquet of wildflowers clutched in one hand. His expression was wistful, almost lovesick. Ichabod, she thought. It had to be.

Near the center, a young woman stood framed in warm light, her gown soft blue against the golden fields—Katrina Van Tassel, no doubt. Her beauty had been rendered with care: delicate jawline, amused eyes, the ghost of a smile. She looked like a secret being kept.

But in the far-left corner, just at the edge of the canvas where the brushwork faded into shadows, something felt off.

A figure stood cloaked in black. Barely more than a silhouette, like the artist hadn't finished—or hadn't meant for it to be noticed. But there it was: the dark curve of a shoulder, a hand half-gloved, and the glint of something metallic near the hip. A sword hilt?

Evelyn narrowed her eyes. The figure's posture didn't match the warmth of the gathering. It was rigid, watchful. Out of place.

She glanced down at the nameplate again. Beneath the title, in tiny lettering almost too faint to read, was a second line:

"Commissioned by Brom Van Brunt. Subjects include the Van Tassel family, Mr. Ichabod Crane, and invited guest— Reverend M. Bollen."

The name stirred something in her memory. She'd seen it earlier in the archives—a margin note on a deed transfer, barely legible: M. Bollen – ceremonial overseer / rites of soil sanctification.

Soil sanctification? She frowned. Was that just a quaint religious phrase or something older?

She pulled out her phone and took a photo of the brass plate and the corner of the painting.

Then she stepped back, heart ticking faster.

"Who exactly were you, Reverend Bollen, … and what were you doing at that harvest gathering?"

Evelyn lingered another beat, eyes tracing the outline of the shadowy figure in the painting once more. The name Bollen repeated itself in her thoughts like a whisper caught on the wind—familiar, unsettling, and completely out of place in what should have been a celebratory family portrait.

Her phone buzzed in her pocket: 7:43 p.m.

The fog outside had thickened again, pressing up against the windows like a living thing.

A low rumble echoed in the quiet hallway. Evelyn blinked, hand drifting to her stomach.

Right. She hadn't eaten since that morning—and even then, she'd been too distracted to finish more than half her sandwich. Her body was quick to remind her that adrenaline didn't count as a food group.

She exhaled and turned from the painting, rubbing a hand over her face. The weight of the day was finally starting to press in—between the near-accident, the rushed escape from the city, the inheritance she hadn't asked for, and now a centuries-old mystery creeping out of local folklore … she needed a moment to breathe.

Her stomach grumbled again.

"Yes, yes. I hear you," she muttered to herself.

She returned upstairs slowly, her limbs heavy from the walk and her thoughts heavier still. As she reached her door, she stopped.

A small brown paper bag sat just outside on the floor. A folded slip of paper was tucked neatly beneath it, written in careful, familiar handwriting:

Had a great time today — hope we can do it again soon. Thought you might need something sweet to get you through moving to your next location.

– Peter

Evelyn picked it up and stepped into her room. The scent of lavender and cedar greeted her like an old quilt as she shut the door behind her.

She set the note aside and opened the bag, peeling back the wax paper to reveal two turnovers — golden and still faintly warm. The smell of cinnamon and baked apple filled the room like something from a memory she couldn't place.

She took a bite without thinking, too tired to resist.

The crust flaked perfectly beneath her teeth, the filling warm and rich. Her eyes widened slightly. Dang. She hadn't expected it to be that good.

A smile crept across her face — genuine, brief, and entirely earned by sugar and spice.

Still chewing, she crossed to her suitcase and began folding the last of her things, pastry in one hand, thoughts still churning — but just a little sweeter now. The gesture was simple. Sincere, even. And for a second, she let herself believe this town might be as harmless as Peter made it seem.

But she couldn't afford to get comfortable. She couldn't forget why she was here. Why she was hiding. Why her real name — her real life — wasn't something she could afford to share.

And she sure as hell wasn't about to fall for some small-town romantic. She'd built a career clawing her way up through the noise and grit of the city. She'd earned her place, bled for it. There was no version of her that traded all that for apple turnovers and pretty smiles.

A year ago, this would've been nothing — just a friendly neighbor, a warm pastry, a good day. Now even kindness felt like something to brace against.

She zipped up her bag and exhaled. "Okay."

She checked her cell for any missed calls or messages. Her lock screen held no notifications. Her boss knew that she wouldn't be able to reach her, and Detective Stanley said he would only message her if there were any updates.

She nodded to herself. "No news is good news." She returned her cell to her jacket pocket, reminding herself there was plenty here to distract her.

That painting. That name — Bollen. It wasn't finished with her. She could feel it in her bones, quiet and certain. This town held secrets.

Her gaze slid to the window, where fog clung to the glass like breath on a mirror, softening the edges of fall trees into long, watchful shadows.

She grabbed her bag, slung it over her shoulder, and stepped out into the hallway—ready to sift the truth of her family's legacy from the local myths and whispered warnings. At least it would keep her mind busy.

Chapter 6
Hollow House

The cab's tires hissed against the wet gravel as it pulled away, taillights swallowed by fog that clung low over the trees. Evelyn stood there — alone now — key cold in her hand and rain softening to a misty drizzle.

The cottage stood like a relic from another time, tucked behind a crooked gate and a stretch of overgrown hedges. From a distance, it looked charming in that old-world, hand-painted postcard kind of way. But up close … it was tired.

The shutters hung uneven on rusted hinges. Paint peeled from the trim in long, flaking strips. Ivy choked the siding in thick coils, climbing into the eaves like it meant to claim the whole structure. The roof sagged ever so slightly near the chimney, and one of the porch steps bowed under the weight of time.

She had expected quaint. Worn, maybe. But this? This was more decay than charm. Evelyn shifted her bag higher on her shoulder and let out a slow breath. The air smelled of moss and old wood, the kind of scent that clung to basements and buried things. Still, she stepped forward. The house may have been forgotten, but it was hers now, and she had nothing else to occupy her time.

"Okay," she murmured. "You're just a house."

But even saying it didn't make it true.

She inhaled deeply and stepped forward.

The key turned with a slow, rusty click.

Inside, the air was still. Cool. Undisturbed.

Her boots echoed faintly on the wooden floor as she closed the door behind her. Dust danced in the beams of receding sunlight pouring through the tall front windows. The entry opened into a narrow sitting room with a faded settee, two mismatched armchairs, and a fireplace framed in heavy brick. Bookshelves lined one wall, and a crooked painting of a river bend hung above a writing desk.

She moved slowly, fingers brushing over surfaces as if they might dissolve. The place felt ... preserved. Not in a curated way, but like time itself had folded around it and left it untouched.

"Someone lived here," she whispered. "Really lived here."

She didn't need a town story to feel that something had happened here.

Past the sitting room, the kitchen was even smaller. Worn tile. Deep sink. A wooden table with two chairs. A kettle sat on the stove like it had been waiting.

Upstairs, the floor groaned beneath her boots — each step another complaint from a house long forgotten. Two bedrooms and a large bath, complete with an antique vanity and a clawfoot tub. Everything else was sparse. Basic. Dust clung to every surface like it had roots. Cracked plaster peeled in long, curling strips. Floorboards shifted underfoot with soft, unsettling pops.

This wasn't a home. Not yet. Just bones and cobwebs.

Back downstairs, the narrow staircase felt steeper in reverse. Evelyn paused in the entry hall, letting the space settle around her. Maybe she had checked out of the inn too soon.

A creak echoed from deeper in the house, somewhere near the kitchen.

She stiffened, every instinct flaring. Probably just the house settling — but she went to check anyway.

She stopped beside the small dining table, scanning the room. Nothing looked disturbed … and yet something about the layout tugged at her attention. Subtle. Wrong.

When she turned to a shadowed alcove behind the pantry, she saw it: a faint square etched into the floorboards.

She crouched.

A cellar door.

The air around the seam was colder. Not the usual damp chill — but something heavier. Older. The kind of cold that made the hairs along her arms lift without warning.

She narrowed her eyes. "If something jumps out at me, I swear …"

Flicking on her flashlight, she aimed the beam at the tarnished brass latch. It stuck under her grip, old and stubborn, but with both hands braced, she pried the door open. The hinges groaned in protest.

A gust of air rolled up from the dark below — damp and cold.

She leaned forward, shining her light into the pit.

Cobwebs. Dust. Wooden rungs vanishing into shadow like the teeth of some waiting thing.

Common sense whispered: Nope.

She set the phone down, tied her hair back into a rough ponytail, and gave the darkness one last look.

"This is a terrible idea," she muttered.

And climbed down anyway.

The basement smelled of damp earth and cedar. The walls were stone, and the air hung with silence so thick it felt alive. Toward the back was an old trunk, iron-cornered, half-covered by a moth-eaten blanket.

Evelyn crouched.

The latch stuck, but she pried it open.

Inside were wrapped bundles — old papers, leather-bound books, letters sealed with red wax. At the very bottom, she uncovered a thick, weathered journal. The cover read: *I. Crane.*

Her throat tightened. She stared at the journal like it might speak first.

"Ichabod Crane," she murmured. "I guess we're going to get to know each other after all."

She opened the first page. The handwriting was careful, formal.

September 2nd, 1723. The air today turned sharp. Autumn is near. My dreams continue to stir with symbols I dare not describe aloud....

She turned another page. Then another. The entries were full of quiet dread — of something seen, something sensed.

September 14th, 1723

While clearing brush near the southern edge of the field, I unearthed a curious stone – dull gray, heavy for its size, and colder than the surrounding earth. At first, I mistook it for tarnished silver, but its texture is strange ... resistant to scratch or fire. Even the blacksmith could not melt a flake of it.

I've never seen a metal like this.

I've wrapped a sample and will deliver it to Mr. Corbett in Tarry Town for further examination. If it is indeed a new substance – or some rare refinement – it may be worth something. Perhaps even enough to secure Katrina's hand.

And yet ... I feel uneasy. The soil was warm above it. Almost feverish. And last night, I dreamt again of black hooves pounding the earth and a rider with no face.

"Something had you scared, but I doubt very much it was an apparition," she thought aloud.

Behind her, something thudded upstairs.

Evelyn froze.

She waited, breath caught in her throat – listening.

Silence.

Her shoulders sagged slightly. Probably just the house settling. Or wind. Or –

She didn't finish the thought. Instead, she returned the journal to the trunk, closing the lid with more force than necessary. Not out of fear – at least, not the kind she wanted to admit – but instinct. Something primal had kicked up in her chest.

The cellar door groaned as she shut it, the latch sticking before finally giving with a click. She leaned her weight into it, like she could force the house back into stillness.

But when she turned toward the hallway mirror, she blinked.

There — over her shoulder in the reflection.

A shadow. Tall. Human-shaped. Moving into the next room.

Her heart slammed against her ribs.

"Hey!" she called out, voice sharp.

She darted into the room just as cold air slid down the back of her neck like an icy hand. She spun around.

And froze. A figure stood in the far corner. Still. Watching. He wasn't part of the shadows — he cast them. Too solid to ignore. Too silent to explain.

Her breath hitched.

Logic clawed for control. You're sleep-deprived. Stressed. Seeing things. But she wasn't. Because when she blinked … he was still there. Just for a second. Then — gone.

She staggered back a step, pulse thundering.

No footsteps. No door creak. Just empty space.

Except — there.

Movement.

The figure appeared again, half-seen in the threshold. As if he'd stepped out from between two layers of time. Evelyn's breath caught in her throat. They locked eyes — his gaze impossibly sharp for something not supposed to exist.

Then he took two slow, deliberate steps toward her.

She backed away, boots catching on the uneven floorboards. She stumbled, nearly falling.

His expression changed — shock rippling across his face like wind over water.

"You can see me?" His voice cracked the silence, low and

trembling.

Evelyn's mouth opened, but no sound came at first. Her brain was scrambling for sense — reason — denial.

But still … "Yes," she whispered. "I can."

His chest rose with a sharp inhale, his disbelief mirroring her own. "And you can hear me?"

"I … yes," she said, more firmly this time, though her body remained frozen in place.

He stepped closer — cautious, as if doing his best not to frighten her off. He extended a hand, tentative, like a man reaching for warmth after centuries in cold.

"This can't be happening," she murmured, half to him, half to herself.

Her heart was sprinting now, every nerve screaming that she was too far from the door. So she turned and bolted — but the floor betrayed her. A warped board gave beneath her foot, sending her off-balance. Her heel caught the rug, and she pitched forward, arms flailing.

The fireplace loomed — brick and iron, jagged and unyielding — rushing up to meet her.

But it never did.

Arms caught her midair, firm and unshakable, halting her with a jolt that stole the breath from her lungs.

She didn't fall. She floated.

Then the world shifted — her body turned slowly, like she was weightless. Guided.

And there he was. Those eyes — deep, storm-dark blue — met hers up close now, clear and sharp as lightning on a winter night. There was something in them that hadn't been there a moment ago.

Worry.

Then — darkness.

She came to slowly, the fog in her mind clearing one breath at a time. A warm ache pulsed at the base of her skull, but she wasn't lying on the cold floor. Cushions. She blinked, staring up at the soft light filtering through the parlor curtains. Dust floated lazily in the shafts of moonlight, and the faint scent of lavender and cedar filled her lungs.

The settee.

She was on the velvet settee in the front sitting room.

How the —

She sat up too quickly. A wave of dizziness crashed over her, but she powered through it, eyes scanning the room.

Her leather bags still sat in the entry, exactly where she'd left them. Her coat had been draped over her like a blanket.

A chill unfurled down her spine.

She looked down at herself. No bruises. No injuries. She hadn't hit the fireplace. She should have.

She remembered falling.

She remembered him.

The figure. The voice.

You can see me? His words surfaced like bubbles from a dream.

Evelyn swallowed hard, one hand pressing to her chest. Her heart galloped under her palm. Not a dream. Not a hallucination. Something — someone — had caught her. And then carried her here.

She glanced toward the stairs. Then back at her bags. Had he …? No. Could a ghost do that?

She rose on shaky legs. The room felt too still. The silence wasn't peaceful — it was poised. Listening. If this was Sleepy Hollow's idea of a welcoming committee, she was going to need stronger coffee. Or a priest. Or both.

But one thing was certain: Someone had kept her from cracking her skull open like an egg on that fireplace. She rubbed her arms, suddenly aware of the cold. The chill was cooler than it should have been — even for a fall night.

"What is going on in this house?"

She grabbed her jacket and shrugged it on, fingers stiff with leftover adrenaline. For one reckless second, she considered marching back to the inn — ghosts, darkness, and muddy ditches be damned.

She crossed to the window and peeled back the curtain.

The woods pressed close to the cottage, dense and unwelcoming. Gnarled branches clawed at the sky, black silhouettes against a deeper black. Mist slithered through the underbrush like it had a mind of its own, curling over tree roots and winding around the base of the porch. The long dirt lane that snaked toward the village was barely visible — just a pale thread vanishing into the trees. No moonlight. No sound. Not even crickets.

The kind of silence that made you feel watched.

She swallowed.

"I think I'll take my chances here," she muttered, letting the curtain fall shut.

The house might be haunted — but at least it had walls and fewer eyes.

Chapter 7
The Veil Thins

Evelyn sat curled on the edge of the settee, blanket clutched around her shoulders, her eyes tracing the glow of the hallway light like it might vanish if she blinked too long. The silence wasn't true silence — this house didn't do quiet. It creaked and settled like it had lungs of its own.

Somewhere above her, the pipes groaned. Outside, dry leaves skittered across the porch in quick bursts — sharp and scratchy, like fingernails on wood.

She hadn't turned off a single light.

Every whisper of wind against the eaves, every shift in shadow made her spine stiffen. The mirror was still. But she didn't trust it.

When her phone rang, the sound ripped through the stillness. She jolted upright, heart hammering as she crossed the room in a half-stumble. Her hand dove into her purse, rummaging past her wallet and keys. The screen flared to life just as she found it, buzzing in her hand like it knew she was already on edge.

Detective Stanley.

She swiped to answer.

"Hello?"

"Ms. Crane," he said—tense, clipped. "I didn't wake you, did I?"

"No, I—" She rubbed at her eyes. "What's going on?"

"We received a tip an hour ago. One of Russo's men was seen heading north, just off the interstate."

Her stomach dropped. "That's this direction," she said slowly, bracing a hand against the wall. Her mind raced with thoughts. "My car—it's still out there. In a ditch. Near a highway exit just outside Sleepy Hollow."

Stanley muttered a curse. "Then we've got a problem."

"Do you think he'll recognize it? The car?"

"If he's any good. Yeah. He might not know where you are yet, but that car is a blinking beacon if he passes it."

She could already see it—her life unraveling. Again. Faster this time.

"Alright," he continued. "Stay put. Lay low. I'll call the local tow company myself and get that car off the road before sunup. Don't open the door to anyone. Keep your phone on you. Understood?"

"Yes," she whispered, her voice paper-thin. "Thank you."

He hung up before she could say more.

Evelyn lowered the phone. Her chest constricted, tight and aching. She couldn't breathe. She leaned back against the wall, eyes darting to the curtained window as though danger might already be standing there.

The house suddenly felt smaller. Trapped. Everything inside her spiraled — thoughts, breath, heartbeat. The air was too thin. Too sharp.

He's coming. He's coming. He's coming.

She sank to the floor, clutching at her chest, as if she could hold herself together by force. Her lungs fought against her ribs, drawing in shallow, panicked gasps. Her vision blurred.

I can't do this. This can't be happening.

A single tear escaped from the outer corner of her eye.

Above her, looking down, the male figure stood just beyond the threshold of the stairwell, unseen. The sight of her curled on the floor — frightened, unraveling — struck something inside him.

She'd recoiled from him earlier. Fled. He should've let it be. Mortals always ran. Always broke. But she looked small now. Fragile in a way that didn't fit her fire. And that damn tear — He sighed, low and reluctant, then stepped forward, walking through the railing and descending gradually through the open air.

The change was subtle at first. A hush in the room. The air warmed — not by hearth or furnace. A gentle pressure settled across her chest like a steadying hand. Not skin. Not quite. Warmth bloomed beneath her palm. Her breath caught … and then released, a little deeper than before. Then another.

Slower. Surer.

The panic eased its grip, one thread at a time. Her limbs stopped trembling. Her back sank into the wall. Her eyes fluttered shut. She didn't question it. She just let go.

Beside her, the ghost sat in silence.

Not looming. Not hovering. Just there.

His arms rested on his knees, body angled toward her—watchful, quiet, unsure. The flicker of concern in his expression made him almost … human again.

He didn't speak.

Didn't need to.

He stayed until her breathing evened out completely.

Until the weight of the world lifted just enough to let her sleep.

Her head dipped forward as exhaustion pulled her under, breath slowing, limbs heavy. The hardwood floor was unforgiving beneath her, but she barely noticed it anymore. She shifted slightly, trying to lean into the warmth at her side—only there was nothing there.

She fell through him. The chill was instant. A deep, unnatural cold that sank into her shoulder like mist sliding under skin. Her eyes snapped open. She jolted upright with a sharp inhale, one hand braced against the wall to steady herself. Her pulse thundered in her ears. And then she saw him. Seated just beside her, his long legs drawn up, arms resting across his knees—watching her.

He was clearer now. Less flicker, more form. The dim light from the entry lamp glinted off the edges of his coat, but his features were shadowed in quiet restraint. Still. Present. Real in a way ghosts weren't supposed to be.

She stared at him—really stared. Not through him, not past him, but at him. Her breath still shallow but steadying.

He was broad-shouldered and powerfully built beneath

weatherworn 18th-century clothing—breeches and boots dusted with dried earth, a dark waistcoat fitted over a loose, unlaced shirt. The coat he wore was torn at one shoulder, scorched faintly at the hem, as if he'd come from fire—or through it.

His blond curls clung damply to his temples and fell just past his ears, catching the dim light like strands of tarnished gold.

But it was his eyes that rooted her in place—

Ice blue. Piercing. Hollowed by time.

He looked like a man carved from beauty and grief.

"You caught me," she whispered. "Back in the parlor. I should've cracked my skull open."

"Is that a question or a statement?"

"A question, I guess."

He gave a faint nod. "You're the first person in a long time that can see me. I wasn't about to waste that opportunity. Not so soon, anyway."

Evelyn's brows drew together. She couldn't tell if his humor was dry or if he really meant what he said. "You didn't touch me. I didn't feel arms. Just … I stopped."

"Yeah, well," he gestured to himself. "Ghost. I can't touch you. But I can manipulate the environment."

"Then it's real," she murmured. "You're real."

His mouth lifted in the ghost of a smile. "I'm not sure 'real' is the word most would use."

Silence stretched between them, the air tinged with tension and something like fragile awe.

She studied him in the half-light. "You're not just some local legend, are you?"

"No." He paused, then he added with a dry edge, "Though I've been called worse."

Evelyn gave a soft, disbelieving laugh. "And you're not … him, are you? The Horseman?"

His face darkened, the air pulling tighter around them. "No," he said, curt and cold. "I've spent three centuries making sure that monster never takes another innocent."

She blinked. "Then who are you?"

A long silence followed. Something unreadable passed through his expression.

"I'm no one important."

She frowned. "You saved my life. That makes you important to me."

He looked away, jaw tightening. "Names don't mean much anymore."

"I disagree."

His eyes met hers again. Haunted. Weary.

"Washington Silas Irving," he said at last.

His name hit her like a chill gust.

"Irving…" she echoed, stunned. "As in — ?"

"Ichabod Crane's only friend. Seems like that's the only legacy I left behind. The man who vanished on the road the night Ichabod died."

Evelyn tried to swallow the swirl of emotion in her chest. A name passed down in shadowed rumors. A man forgotten by time. And yet — here he was.

"How well did you know Ichabod?"

"'Bout as good as any. Certainly better than the rest of town.

Except perhaps Katrina Van Tassel." He said her name like there was a bad history with it.

Silas's gaze dropped to the floor, but before Evelyn could respond, he stood. The shift in his form stirred the air like a ripple across still water.

"You should rest, Miss …"

She rose unsteadily to her feet, pulse still skipping. "Evelyn."

A pause. Then a small, reluctant nod. "Evelyn."

As she stood, she hesitated. "Why me? Why can I see you?"

His expression turned grim. "That … I don't yet know. But something's changed."

Her spine prickled.

And then he was gone.

Evelyn stood in the silence, the echo of his presence still clinging to the air like static. She stood there for a long while after he vanished. The house creaked and sighed around her, but it wasn't settling noises this time. It was the echo of presence — the unmistakable hum of something lingering just beyond the veil.

Evelyn wrapped her arms around herself, uncertain whether she was colder from the draft or from the ghost who'd just confessed his name to her.

"Washington Silas Irving." She whispered it aloud, testing the shape of it on her tongue. It didn't feel unfamiliar.

"Ichabod Crane's only friend," she repeated softly.

The name should have meant nothing more than a line in a town's ghost story — but it tugged at something buried in her. A hollow that hadn't had a name until now.

Was it fear?

Recognition?

She didn't know.

Her phone vibrated again in her hand — just once. A voicemail from Stanley. The text read, Just letting you know that a local tow truck has picked up your car and they will start working on it for you. I will keep you posted. Stay safe.

Evelyn crossed to the front window and pulled the curtain back just an inch. The woods beyond the cottage were ink-dark. Trees stood like sentinels, their bare arms tangled against the night sky. Fog curled low across the long dirt lane, thickening near the edge where the road vanished into the pines. No headlights. No movement. But her instincts screamed anyway.

He's coming.

She released the curtain, shutting the darkness out.

Silence. And the faint scent of rain, fading fast.

Evelyn exhaled, grabbed a blanket from the back of the settee, and curled into the sofa. She didn't sleep. Not really. But when she closed her eyes, she didn't feel quite as alone.

Chapter 8
The Face in the Headlines

Evelyn woke to silence. Not the unsettling kind she'd come to expect in this house but a quieter quiet — one untouched by ghosts or nightmares. For a moment, she kept her eyes shut, steeling herself. Part of her expected to feel that strange warmth again, that eerie sense of presence. She half-hoped Silas would be there, watching from the corner like he had the night before.

But the room was empty.

She sat up slowly, glancing around. No sign of him. Not that she'd know what to look for. The curtains swayed gently in the morning draft. The room was still and cold but not … haunted. Not exactly.

Maybe it had all been some stress-induced fever dream. Too many secrets. Too little sleep. Her stomach growled.

Right. Food.

Detective Stanley had told her to stay put. Lay low. Don't go anywhere. But hiding was a lot harder on an empty stomach —

and near impossible with a pantry full of nothing but expired baking soda and dust.

She stood and stretched, her spine cracking with a satisfying pop. Crossing to the window, she pulled the curtains open. Gray daylight seeped through the panes. Rain still drizzled lightly, making the world outside look soft and slightly smudged. The storm had passed, but the gloom lingered.

No food. No coffee. No cleaning supplies. No sense of security. Evelyn sighed and grabbed her phone off the charger. She tapped in the number from the crumpled cab receipt still tucked in her coat pocket. After three rings, a voice answered — gravelly and familiar.

"Sleepy Hollow Cabs."

"Hi. It's Evelyn Cr — Cooper," she said quickly. "From last night. I need a ride into town."

"Back to the Inn?"

"No," she said, too fast. "Just the general store. Maybe the market. I won't be long."

A pause. A beat longer than she liked.

"Alright. Vehicle'll be out to you in just a few minutes."

"Perfect," she replied. "I'll be out front in ten."

She hung up and made her way to her bag, already dreading what she'd see in the mirror. Her reflection confirmed her suspicion — smudged eyeliner, sleep-creased cheeks, and haunted eyes.

She pulled a brush through her natural waves and twisted them into a loose, messy bun. It passed for stylish in the city. Hopefully it would do the same here. Grabbing her small makeup bag, she padded to the bathroom, flicked on the light, and gave herself a quick once-over. Concealer, mascara, a sweep of blush. Good enough.

She returned to the front room, pulling on her coat. Her boots thudded dully against the old floorboards as she crossed to the front door. The air on the other side of it felt colder somehow. Not just from the weather—but from something else. That creeping edge of being watched, even when she knew she was alone.

Or thought she was.

She paused with her hand on the doorknob.

"I'll be quick," she murmured to the house, unsure if she was talking to herself … or to someone else entirely.

Then she opened the door and stepped out into the mist.

The cab dropped her off just outside the general store, its chipped green awning fluttering in the breeze. A brass bell chimed overhead as she stepped inside.

It was quaint. One of those small-town staples that sold everything from canned soup to windshield wipers to novelty postcards. The air smelled like cinnamon, motor oil, and something vaguely medicinal. A few older locals milled around, chatting softly with the cashier or browsing through the aisles.

Evelyn kept her head down and grabbed a basket.

Groceries first. Then batteries. Flashlight. Dish soap. Coffee—thank goodness, they had coffee. She loaded up on canned goods, dry pasta, anything that wouldn't spoil. There was something oddly comforting about stocking up, like she could build herself a wall out of nonperishables.

As she turned the corner toward the housewares aisle, her eyes caught on the faint flicker of a TV screen mounted in the sitting nook near the front. It played low, almost muted, showing a local news station with closed captions on. A headline scrolled slowly across the bottom:

RUSSO SYNDICATE INVESTIGATION DEEPENS — MISSING JOURNALIST.

Evelyn stopped cold.

The anchor's voice droned over the noise of scanners and sliding carts. "—latest developments in the Russo crime ring takedown. Federal officials say the organization's top lieutenants are still at large following last month's exposé. The journalist responsible for breaking the story, Evelyn Crane, has not been seen since the release of the article that exposed the Russo family's hidden assets, shell companies, and alleged involvement in several unsolved disappearances."

And then — her face.

Not from her phone or a profile picture. A press photo from her time at the paper. Clean. Professional. Recognizable.

The closed captioning confirmed it:

"...the unidentified woman believed to be connected to the testimony has not been seen since the arraignment two weeks ago. Authorities continue to pursue leads—"

Evelyn quickly turned down the next aisle, pulse thudding in her ears.

No one had noticed. The man near the register was too busy fishing for exact change. A woman in gardening gloves flipped through coupons. No heads turned. No eyes locked.

Still—her palms began to sweat.

She finished shopping at double speed, mentally running down a list of what she still needed. Laundry detergent. Disinfectant. Lightbulbs. A first-aid kit. She was halfway to the register before she realized she hadn't even grabbed bread.

Every time she passed someone, her breath hitched. That old man's glance lasted a beat too long. The cashier gave her a polite smile—but was it too polite? The teenager sweeping the floor had looked up as she passed. Had he recognized her?

The walls of the store felt closer. Thicker.

She paid in cash, her heart pounding, and thanked the cashier with a quick smile she couldn't quite fake. The bell above the door jingled as she pushed her way outside, arms full of grocery bags and nerves shot through with static.

The cab was still parked down the block, hazard lights blinking slowly in the fog. She walked fast, not quite running, but close enough to draw a few looks. Her boots echoed off the cracked sidewalk.

Don't run. Just walk. You're no one here. They're not looking at you.

But the cold certainty sank in all the same.

They would be. Soon.

And now Sleepy Hollow didn't just hold ghosts—it held a journalist with a target on her back.

The cab crunched up the gravel drive, tires groaning in protest as it came to a stop. Evelyn had barely reached for the door handle when Sam, the driver, leapt out of the vehicle with more enthusiasm than she'd mustered all morning.

"I've got it; I've got it," he called cheerfully, already lifting four bags in each hand.

"That's really not necessary—" Evelyn tried, but he was already climbing the front steps.

"Nah, it's no trouble," he said with a grin, his warm baritone practically bouncing off the damp porch beams. "You've got enough to worry about, movin' into this spooky place."

She bit back a sigh and followed him up, groceries in tow.

Sam was tall, broad-shouldered, and somewhere in his late forties, with a face that wore smile lines like well-earned medals. His deep-brown skin glowed with health, and his eyes sparkled beneath the bill of his Sleepy Hollow Cabs cap. He had a voice that made even ghost stories sound like warm bedtime tales—and unfortunately, he had plenty of them.

"I swear, back in high school, me and a few buddies snuck out here one night—just to see if we could catch the Crane ghost. Thought we were real smooth, but I swear on my momma's cornbread, we didn't make it past the porch. Heard one weird sound and sprinted back to the truck like cowards."

He laughed, shaking his head as she slipped the old key from her trouser pocket. It slid into the skeleton keyhole with a soft click.

"I mean, we never saw anything," Sam added, leaning closer, "but we felt it, y'know?"

Evelyn gave a tight smile and opened the door, ushering him inside. "Must've been something in the air."

"Something in the air, alright," he chuckled.

They set the groceries down on the dusty kitchen table, the scent of lemon cleaner and mildew mixing in the air. Sam gave the house a cursory look, stepping briefly into each room on his way back toward the door.

"Still got that old wood smell," he remarked. "Spooky or not, it's got character. Shame nobody ever wanted to stay."

Evelyn followed him to the entry, grateful for the subtle goodbye.

"Thanks again," she said, managing a real smile this time.

"Don't mention it. Call if you need anything. I mean it." He pointed to her. "Anything weird, anything heavy, anything lonely. I'll be around."

With that, he tipped his cap and walked back across the lawn, boots squelching slightly in the soft, rain-soaked grass.

The moment the door shut, Evelyn locked it tight—bolt and all—then leaned against it with a sigh that hollowed her out.

Her body slid to the floor, back pressed to the wood. She pulled her knees in tight and buried her face into them as the tears finally came.

She hadn't cried in the car, or in the market, or even when she saw her own face on the flippin' news. But now, behind locked doors and peeling wallpaper, she let it all crack open.

Her chest heaved, shoulders shaking as the pressure spilled over. The panic attack at the store, the terror of being recognized, the weight of constantly looking over her shoulder. She thought this was what she wanted—exposing monsters, revealing truth, holding evil to the light. But maybe the thrill wasn't worth being hunted for it. Maybe being a headline wasn't the legacy she wanted after all.

A faint draft brushed the back of her neck.

She didn't look up.

"I'm fine," she said to the quiet, voice hoarse. "I'm fine. Just give me a second."

"You don't look fine."

She startled, lifting her tear-streaked face. Silas stood halfway between shadow and light, his figure coalescing near the stairs, arms crossed over his chest like the brooding statue.

His tone wasn't mocking—just blunt. Like he'd long since forgotten how to speak gently and wasn't about to relearn it now.

"You always spy on people when they're falling apart?" she asked, wiping at her face with the back of her sleeve.

His brow lifted. "I'm a ghost. Spying's about all I'm good for."

She let out a wet, broken laugh.

Silas took a step closer, eyes searching her face. "What happened?"

Evelyn shook her head. "Nothing. Everything." She wiped the wet from her cheek. "The news has my face on it. The Russo case—I'm the one who exposed it. That's why I'm here. Hiding. And today I got to watch strangers glance at the TV and almost look back at me."

He said nothing.

Evelyn realized, belatedly, that he probably didn't even know who the Russos were.

Of course he didn't. Why would he?

Her gaze dropped to her lap, fingers twisting together as if they could work the tension out of her nerves.

"Thank you," she finally said. "For last night. You prevented a migraine at the least."

His mouth twitched. "Would've been messy. Blood on the rug, cracked head... and here I thought you might be the one person to try to keep this place livable."

"I'm very considerate that way," she murmured, wiping the last of the tears from her cheeks. "Leave it to me to nearly die in a place that looks like a vintage horror set."

He tilted his head. "I'd argue the parlor has charm."

"Sure. If you like antique trauma."

"Better than modern chaos."

She gave him a side-eye. "You don't even know what modern chaos looks like. Or even just modern for that matter."

Silas shrugged one shoulder. "I know enough to avoid whatever possessed you to buy four different kinds of Pop-Tarts and a lifetime supply of black coffee."

Her mouth dropped open. "Excuse me?"

He nodded toward the bags on the table. "I saw the receipts."

"You went through my bags?"

"I looked. There's a difference."

"You're a ghost, not a TSA agent."

"And yet somehow, I'm the only one here with any sense of threat prevention."

"Oh-ho," she huffed. "Threat prevention, is it?"

"Yep. Because judging by those groceries, you're one bad decision away from culinary catastrophe."

She huffed a laugh despite herself, hands on her hips. "Okay, Mr. Security System. What would you have bought?"

"Something to eat out of would be nice. Matches. Salt. Maybe a crowbar."

She blinked. "A crowbar?"

"You never know."

Evelyn squinted at him, suspicious, then dropped the expression as her train of thought jumped tracks. "Wait—I saw dishes in the cupboard," she said, walking toward the kitchen.

"Sure," he called after her. "If you don't mind consuming small amounts of lead while you eat."

She folded her arms. "So now you're a ghost and a kitchen prepper?"

Silas gave a solemn nod. "Multifaceted haunting. I like to stay relevant."

It was ridiculous. And ridiculous felt like exactly what she needed.

For the first time in a long time, Evelyn laughed—really laughed. A soft, startled sound that pulled the tension out of her shoulders and left her lighter on her feet.

Silas didn't smile, exactly. But the shadows in his expression eased, and that was close enough.

She looked at him, and for a moment, the room didn't feel quite so haunted.

"You're a strange one, Irving."

"Lucky for you," he said, fading slowly from view, "I tend to haunt with charm."

And then he was gone.

No sound. No flicker.

Just … absence.

Evelyn stood there, alone again—but it wasn't the same kind of alone. Not anymore.

She glanced toward the empty space where he'd been, pulse steadying against the echo of his voice. There were still too many questions. About him. About the house. About why she could see him when no one else could. But one truth had started to take root, quiet and unshakable. Silas wasn't just part of this town's past anymore. Something about her being there was causing a shift in the town—and in her.

Chapter 9
Croissants, Coffee, and Ghosts

The sound of rustling fall leaves poured in through the open window. It was a gentle wakening. Muted gray light filtered through the gauzy curtains of the front sitting room, brushing against Evelyn's cheek. She stirred, curled beneath her coat on the settee, limbs stiff from the hardwood beneath her.

Evelyn blinked against the light, unsure what had woken her. Her head throbbed dully from sleep, and her chest felt hollow, like she'd wept through dreams she couldn't remember. She sat up slowly, bracing her hands on the cushion as her gaze swept the quiet.

No sign of him.

She rubbed her hands along her arms, trying to shake the chill that clung to her bones.

The only audible sound was the creak of old wood as the house settled around her. Familiar now. Not comforting. Not yet. Still, her chest no longer clenched like a fist. Her panic hadn't followed her into the dawn. That ... meant something.

She stood, stretching out the aches from her neck and shoulders. The sunlight made the dust in the air shimmer like static. Evelyn crossed the room, eyes flicking once more to the spot where Silas had vanished the night before.

"Thanks," she murmured. "Wherever you are."

She didn't expect a reply.

And none came.

Just the slow, strange calm of a house learning to share its silence.

Then, abruptly, a voice called from the front of the house.

"Evelyn?"

She nearly jumped out of her skin, spinning toward the sound.

"Anybody home?" the voice echoed again.

Her shoulders sagged with recognition. Peter.

She rushed to the front door, wiping possible mascara flakes from under her eyes and doing a quick hair check in the mirror.

"Evelyn?" Peter's voice called again, closer this time—his footsteps creaking on the front porch.

She brushed her hands against her jeans as if trying to rub away the chill clinging to her skin. Her pulse still thrummed unevenly as she made her way through the narrow hallway toward the front door.

The moment she opened it, warm sunlight spilled in—along with Peter's familiar face, all concerned eyes and a hesitant smile.

"Oh, hey! There you are," he said, offering a charming smile. "I hope it's okay to drop in on you. When I heard a young woman in town had purchased the Crane place—" He paused, finally noticing her tense posture and pale complexion. "You okay? You look like you've seen a ghost."

Evelyn let out a shaky laugh, too quick. "Yeah, I just woke up. And, um..." She shook her head and smiled faintly. "I'm alright. Um, how did you hear about me being here?"

Peter raised a brow but didn't press. "I was at Maddie's Coffee shop and overheard a neighbor say someone had finally purchased the old Crane place."

"And you just assumed it was me?"

"Well, it wasn't that hard to guess. No one already living here bought it, or everyone would've been talking about that person considering it beforehand. And you're the only stranger in town." He pressed his lips together, a little sheepish. "Sounds nosy, doesn't it?"

"Just a little," she teased.

He grinned. "I brought coffee and breakfast croissants. Thought you might need reinforcements."

She stepped aside, forcing a smile. "Come on in."

As he entered, Evelyn cast her gaze over the area — wondering if Silas would pop in. But rooms held only furniture.

"Welcome to Crane Cottage."

Peter glanced around as they stepped into the narrow entryway. "Definitely scarier on the inside," he teased.

"I expected it to be more ... maintained," Evelyn said, frowning. "Considering the previous owner only just passed."

Peter chuckled. "No one's actually been inside in a long time — aside from a few curious teenagers hoping to spot a ghost."

Evelyn's brows lifted. "Ghosts, huh?"

"Don't look so worried. I'm sure the only residents left are a few spiders and the occasional rodent."

She deadpanned, "Honestly? I think I'd prefer the ghosts."

Evelyn stepped into the sitting room, eyeing the layer of dust that clung to everything like a second skin. A small round table stood near the window, its surface cluttered with a tarnished candlestick, a cracked vase, and a stack of yellowed magazines warped with time.

"I guess we'll have to earn our breakfast," she muttered, brushing cobwebs from the chair nearest her.

Peter followed her in, already setting the coffee tray down on the least dusty corner of the table. "Got any napkins, or are we going full pioneer style?"

Evelyn chuckled. "Pioneer it is."

She began clearing the table, carefully lifting each object and placing it on the windowsill. Peter joined her, grabbing a dry corner of his flannel shirt to wipe at the surface.

"Charming," he said, grimacing as he coughed through the dust. "I give it two stars for ambiance. Great lighting, questionable hygiene."

"I'll be sure to leave a guest book for reviews," Evelyn replied, dragging out a second chair and brushing it off.

They sat across from each other as morning light filtered through the lace curtains — thin, faded things that softened the sharp lines of the worn-down room.

Peter passed her a steaming paper cup with a knowing smile. "New flavor today. Brown sugar cinnamon oat milk latte. Thought you might like it."

Evelyn blinked, surprised. "You keep picking things I wouldn't order in a million years."

"And yet..." He tilted his head, grinning.

She took a cautious sip — and closed her eyes. Smooth, warm, with a faint sweetness that clung to the back of her tongue. Cozy but not cloying.

How does he do this? she wondered.

"I've ordered black coffee for years and thought I was content. But you show up with these unexpected little comforts, and suddenly I'm not sure what I've been missing," she said, smirking behind her cup, "I'll admit it. That's really good."

He raised his own cup in a silent toast. "And there you have it! Victory tastes like cinnamon."

They ate in easy quiet for a moment, the distant caw of a crow echoing through the trees beyond the window. But Evelyn's gaze kept flicking to the hallway and adjoining kitchen.

Peter leaned back in his chair, watching her. "You sure you're okay? You've got that look again."

Evelyn hesitated — her mouth opened, but the truth felt too wild to say aloud. I met Silas Irving. He's a friendly ghost. Not to mention good looking.

"I'm just ... anxious. There are a few things I forgot to get at the hardware store yesterday," she said finally. "This place needs a lot."

Peter nodded, taking another bite of his croissant. "Yeah, you'll need half the shop and probably a tetanus shot."

Evelyn huffed a laugh. "Thanks for the vote of confidence."

"I'm just saying, this place has personality. You might want to carry pepper spray in case the wallpaper attacks."

She rolled her eyes but couldn't stop the smile tugging at her lips. There was something disarming about the way Peter joked—like he wasn't trying to charm her, and somehow that made him even more charming.

He leaned back in his chair, stretching slightly. "Tell you what. After we finish here, I'll take you to the housewares shop in town. It's nothing fancy, but they've got paint, lightbulbs, and enough duct tape to hold this place together until you can bring in actual help."

"Do I look like I'm made of contractor money?"

Peter grinned. "No, but you look like someone who could boss one around with enough caffeine."

She raised her cup in a mock toast. "I'll take that as a compliment."

"It was. And besides, Bruce—he runs the shop—loves helping new people settle in. If he thinks you're restoring this place, he'll probably try to give you half the inventory for free. Just smile, nod, and pretend to care about plumbing."

Evelyn arched a brow. "That's your advice?"

"Absolutely. And as a fallback, just tell him I say you're good for it. Works every time."

She studied him for a moment—his easy grin, the way he hadn't hesitated to show up this morning, coffee in hand, just because he sensed she might need it. She barely knew him, and yet ... there was something steady about Peter Van Tassel. Something kind. Maybe too kind. No matter how much she tried to let her walls fall around him, something in her gut wouldn't relent.

She looked away quickly, folding her pastry wrapper with more attention than necessary.

"Alright," she said. "After breakfast, I'm all yours."

He blinked then smirked. "Well. That escalated quickly."

Heat crept into her cheeks. "You know what I meant."

"I did. But I wasn't going to miss the opportunity."

She shook her head, laughing softly as she stood to gather the trash. "Come on, Romeo. Let's go meet this Bruce guy before the wallpaper really does attack."

Peter followed, still grinning. "My hero moment will come. Just wait."

But behind them, in the corner of the sitting room, a shadow shifted.

A figure stood near the window—tall, still, and almost translucent—watching them with a quiet intensity.

Silas.

She didn't turn. She didn't notice.

And he made no move to be seen.

His gaze was set on Peter, and it wasn't one of admiration.

Chapter 10
What Haunts Us

The day had passed in a blur of dust, laughter, and the clatter of broom handles. Over the last couple of weeks, Evelyn and Peter had settled into a rhythm—each day blending into the next as they worked side by side to bring the old cottage back to life. It had started with a quick supply run to the housewares shop in town, but that had turned into days of cleaning, rearranging, and uncovering forgotten nooks in the house that hadn't seen daylight in decades.

Each morning, Peter showed up at her doorstep like clockwork, bearing some new flavor of coffee and a fresh pastry from the bakery—pumpkin walnut scones, maple pecan muffins, even a croissant once so buttery it nearly made her emotional. Evelyn, who'd once thrived on nothing but black coffee and adrenaline, found herself looking forward to his ridiculous food commentary almost as much as the caffeine.

Her car had finally come back from the mechanic, the

engine now humming like a contented cat. But it hadn't done much more than take up space in the driveway. With Peter always around and eager to help, there hadn't been a real need to drive anywhere.

She was settling in.

Small-town life wasn't what she'd pictured for herself, but it had started to grow on her — mostly because of the company. Peter, during the day, with his rolled-up sleeves and persistent optimism.

And Silas, in the early hours before sunrise or in the fragile quiet before sleep claimed her. He came when the house was still and the world outside was draped in mist. Their conversations had grown longer, less spectral and more... intimate. He listened and somehow understood the things she didn't say out loud. She felt seen by him in a way that made her question the loneliness she hadn't realized she'd been carrying.

There was a gravity to their connection — a strange, impossible closeness that defied explanation. He hadn't asked who she was beyond her first name, and she hadn't offered. Somehow, with Silas, it felt like names and titles didn't matter. Only presence. Only truth. And yet, despite the hours shared, she knew he didn't suspect the truth about her last name. Not yet.

Silas never appeared when Peter was there. Evelyn had started to assume it was some kind of ghostly boundary — one that made sense in its own strange way. But tonight was different.

Now the sun had long dipped behind the trees, and they sat on the floor of the sitting room, paper containers spread out between them like a haphazard picnic. Local takeout from the diner—burgers and sweet potato fries, some kind of mystery pie for dessert—washed down with fizzy bottled root beer. A fire crackled in the hearth, soft light flickering across the walls. The scent of cedar and spices hung in the air.

They were laughing about something ridiculous—probably her poor attempt at folding the laundry Peter had insisted on doing for her earlier—when the moment shifted.

Evelyn reached for another fry at the same time Peter did. Their hands brushed. The laughter faded, and she looked up to find his eyes already on her.

The warmth in the room suddenly had little to do with the fire.

Peter leaned in, intertwining his fingers with hers—light, lingering—like he wasn't sure whether to pull away or hold on. Her pulse fluttered beneath his touch, and she leaned into it, their shoulders brushing. For a moment, the room stilled, suspended in the quiet, magnetic pull between them.

Then—

The fire blew out.

Not fizzled. Not crackled and dimmed.

Blew out.

A soft whoosh echoed in the room, and the light vanished, plunging them into shadow.

Peter blinked, startled. "Okay.... That's not normal."

He rolled over onto his knees and reached for the matches on the hearth. Across the room, just beyond the reach of moonlight leaking through the curtains, a shape lingered.

Evelyn nearly jumped.

Silas.

He stood half-shadowed, as if not entirely part of this world — but this time, his presence felt colder. Sharper. The air around him practically hummed. And his gaze wasn't on her.

It was on Peter.

She stiffened, caught in that sudden tightrope between instinct and confusion. Silas had never appeared when Peter was around. Never crossed that line.

Until now.

For a fleeting second, she wondered if it was jealousy — the way his eyes tracked Peter's movements. But no. This wasn't about affection. Her brow furrowed. The atmosphere itself had shifted, like the room no longer belonged to them.

It belonged to him.

And he didn't want Peter here.

"Don't worry about it," Evelyn said quickly, her hand landing gently on Peter's arm. "Really. It's fine. I'm actually pretty tired."

Peter paused, watching her with mild concern. "You sure? I can get it going again."

"I'm sure." She offered a tired smile, already rising to her feet. "It's been a long day."

He stood, too, brushing crumbs from his hands. "Alright. But tomorrow, I'm showing up with cinnamon rolls. I've been told they have actual healing properties."

"I'll believe it when I taste it."

"Oh — shoot. I just remembered I have a few things to do at the inn first."

"You know you can take a break from helping any time, Peter. No need to make excuses," she teased, nudging his shoulder.

"Ha," he mock-laughed. "No, really—just a couple things to handle, but I'm still coming. Might be closer to noon-ish."

Evelyn shrugged. "Works for me. There's plenty to keep me busy."

They exchanged soft goodnights at the door. Peter hesitated for just a second, eyes lingering on hers—but then he turned and disappeared into the night.

As soon as the door clicked shut, Evelyn turned back into the sitting room.

Silas was still there.

The shadows clung to him like fog on a grave.

She took a slow breath and stepped toward him, her voice low but unwavering. "What was all of that about?"

He shook his head and looked away.

Evelyn crossed her arms. "Just say it, Silas. What do you have against Peter?"

Silas didn't meet her eyes. He stood near the window, where the moonlight caught in his hair, casting a shimmer over his features. "It isn't about Peter."

"That's a lie," she snapped. "Every time his name comes up, you go cold. And not just your usual dead-guy cold. Worse."

A flicker of a smile ghosted over his lips. "Dead-guy cold?"

"Don't deflect." Evelyn took a step toward him. "You don't get to haunt me and then pick and choose what truths I'm allowed to know."

Silas's jaw clenched. "You wouldn't understand."

"Try me."

His eyes flashed, blue and distant as frost. "The Van Tassels and I have history. None of it good."

"You've got to give me more than that," she said with annoyance. "Did they steal your wheat? Burn down your mill? What?"

His mouth tightened, but he didn't answer.

"Oh, come on," she pressed. "You expect me to believe you can materialize out of thin air, stalk me through every creaking hallway of this town, and glare daggers at Peter like he insulted your ghostly honor—yet I'm not allowed to ask why?"

Silas turned away, hands curling at his sides. "It's not about him, Evelyn. He's just a shadow of the legacy his bloodline left behind. They covered up things that should've never been buried. Protected monsters. Unleashed dark legends."

"That sounds exactly like something I should know." Her voice rose. "If I'm caught in this, too, if you keep showing up every time something unexplainable happens, then I deserve answers."

"You deserve peace." He spun around, suddenly fierce. "You deserve to live without this weight pressing on your chest every night. Without looking over your shoulder. At least, no more than you already are. You're already running scared."

He was talking about the Russos.

Evelyn stiffened.

She only knew what she'd seen on TV or caught in tense blips from late-night radio reports. Cases like that—organized crime, contract killers—could drag through the courts for months, sometimes years. But she'd done her part. She'd told the truth. Turned over every document, every shady transaction, every ounce of proof she could gather while the walls were still closing in.

Detective Stanley's last message had been hopeful, almost reassuring. Almost. "Won't be much longer," he'd said. "They'll be behind bars before winter."

But until she saw them in cuffs on the news, until they stayed there, Evelyn didn't feel safe setting foot back in the city.

Perhaps not even then.

"No, I'm not," she lied unconvincingly.

Silas narrowed his eyes. "You forget—I don't just hear what you say. I feel it. Your fear is loud, Evelyn. It clings to you."

He began to pace, his steps uneven, taut with frustration and helplessness. "You cry in your sleep. I hear your heart race the moment terror sinks its claws into you. That's why I don't tell you."

She stared at him, stunned—not by the words but by the raw intensity behind them. His concern wrapped around her like a second skin—unexpected, unshakable, and all too real.

Silas turned away, his jaw tight. "You think I enjoy watching this happen to you? Knowing I can't stop it?" His voice dropped, rough and ragged. "Every night, I listen to you battle shadows—and I'm useless. I hate seeing you haunted by something I can't touch, something I can't protect you from."

He paused then looked back at her over his shoulder, his voice low and weighted with quiet ache. "If I had breath in my lungs and blood in my veins, I'd spend both keeping you safe."

A beat of silence passed between them.

"You think silence is safety," she said, voice trembling now —
not just from anger but from the raw hurt he'd unearthed. "But
all it's done is leave me alone in the dark."

Silas didn't move. Didn't blink. For a moment, he looked
carved from the same stone as the tombstones he lingered near.

"I was alone, too," he said softly. "That night on the path
home. After the Horseman … I just kept thinking to myself, 'If
only I had just kept my mouth shut. If only I just walked away
that night.'"

Her breath caught. "What did they do to you?"

His eyes met hers — haunted, hollow, and soaked in a past
that refused to stay buried. "The curse."

That single word seemed to drain the room of warmth.

Evelyn's mouth parted, but no words came.

Silas took a step back, as if saying more might shatter
something sacred. "They didn't just protect monsters, Evelyn.
They made them."

She shivered. "And Peter?"

A pause.

"There's a small chance he might not know," Silas said.
"But if this were still my time — if the world hadn't changed —
he would. Back then, things like this … were passed down
like heirlooms. People like that …" — his voice darkened — "No
amount of goodness can scrub the blood from their name."

Evelyn took a shaky breath, her thoughts racing. "You really
believe that? That someone's doomed by their bloodline?"

His expression didn't waver. "It's not belief. It's experience.
There are exceptions … but they're rare."

She shook her head slowly. "Peter isn't like that. He's kind. He's steady. He's never given me a reason not to trust him."

"That's how it begins," Silas said, voice sharp as splintering ice. "That's how they began, too. Warm smiles. Gentle hands. Lies wrapped in silk and whispered just low enough to keep you from seeing the fire at your feet."

"You don't know him," she said, but it came out softer now. Less certain.

Silas stepped closer, and the air between them pulled tight, like a storm holding its breath.

"No," he said. "But I know what's buried beneath this house. I know the power of old sins. And I know the Van Tassels were the ones who broke the Horseman's chains and beckoned him back from purgatory."

Evelyn gave a look of disbelief. "I don't believe in headless specters—"

"You probably didn't believe in ghosts before we met either," he retorted.

She held up a hand. "Even if you're right, that was centuries ago."

Silas tilted his head. "Then why does he still ride?"

"Is he?" she doubted.

Silas threw up his hands and turned away.

"I'm not asking you to hate him," Silas said. "I'm suggesting you be careful. Because whatever's stirring—it's waking up fast."

Evelyn stared at him, torn between fear and fury, confusion and compassion. "Then help me understand. Stop pushing me away and help me."

His eyes searched hers, long and hard. But instead of answering, Silas turned and vanished into shadow, leaving her with nothing but the hollow space he'd occupied.

Evelyn exhaled through her nose, sharp and frustrated, and turned back toward the blanket on the floor where dinner sat.

She gathered the plates and glasses, stacking them just so, so they wouldn't roll as she walked to the kitchen sink.

"Who would've guessed ghosts could be so darn stubborn," she muttered.

The scrape of silverware, the clink of ceramic—small, steady sounds that helped keep her grounded. But her thoughts wouldn't stop circling. Each dish she rinsed only cleared more room in her head for questions.

She didn't have answers. Not about Silas. Not about Peter. Not about the things she'd been told to leave alone. But she wouldn't. Not for herself but to bring Silas peace. Perhaps that was why he hadn't been able to move on.

She yawned.

Her excuse to Peter wasn't entirely a lie. She was tired.

Investigating further into Silas' past would have to wait. At least for now.

Chapter 11
History & Inheritance

Evelyn hauled two overstuffed trash bags out the front door, the plastic crinkling loudly in the quiet morning air. Her breath came in faint clouds, the last remnants of the cool night clinging to the sleepy little street. Her arms ached, but it was nothing compared to the heaviness lingering in her chest.

She hadn't slept much. Not after the previous night's conversation.

Silas's voice still echoed in her mind, cold and desperate. They didn't just protect monsters, Evelyn. They made them. And that look on his face—somewhere between grief and guilt—had clung to her long after the shadows swallowed him.

She hadn't seen him since.

But that didn't mean he wasn't there.

Silas had a way of watching without being seen. Sometimes, she could feel it—a brush of cold down her spine, a flicker in the corner of her eye. But today? Nothing.

He was giving her space ... or avoiding her.

She swung open the gate to the rickety fence and tossed the bags into the cans with a grunt just as the mail truck slowed in front of the crooked fence — or what was left of it.

The driver leaned out the window. "I'm looking for an Evelyn — "

"I'm Evelyn," she called, brushing a strand of hair out of her face.

"Well, it's nice to finally meet you, ma'am!" he said, tipping his cap with a warm smile.

He climbed out, opened the back of the truck, and retrieved a cardboard box.

"Mr. Fenn asked me to bring this by during my route."

"Mr. Fenn?" she repeated, puzzled.

"Gregory. The county clerk ..."

"Oh!" Her eyebrows lifted in recognition. "Oh, shoot. Right. I forgot all about going back to grab this. Thank you," she said, accepting the box.

"I'm Ernest Knickerbocker," he added, offering a hand.

Evelyn shifted the box into her left arm and shook his hand. "Nice to meet you, Ernest. I appreciate you bringing this by. I feel bad. I was supposed to grab that weeks ago."

"Oh, sure," he said with a wave. "It's a small town. We all help each other out around here."

Evelyn nodded, her expression softening.

"In fact," he continued, "I'm a bit of a handyman on the side. If you're ever in need of help with the house ..."

"Really? I mean, I can't pay you much — "

"No worry. I come cheap."

She laughed. "That would be great. I have no idea what I'm doing. I've mostly just been clearing out old junk and debris, but if you have time to look at electrical and plumbing sometime, I'd really appreciate it."

"Yeah, I can do that," he said, already walking toward the house.

"Oh—I didn't mean right now. I don't want to disrupt your route."

"Eh, it can wait. Might as well take a look now. If there's anything I need to pick up from Bruce's shop, I can grab it on the way through."

"Okay...." Evelyn glanced back at the mail truck then down the street, half-expecting to see an angry resident waiting for their mail. But no one was around.

"Okay, come on in," Evelyn said, shifting the box and nudging the front door open with her shoulder.

Ernest followed close behind, eyes already scanning the trim, the floorboards, the weathered hinges of the screen door. "This place has character," he said, stepping inside and immediately veering toward the baseboards. "Wow. Original molding. Most folks would paint right over this without even noticing the detail."

Evelyn blinked, still holding the box. "Do you want a tour?"

"Oh, yeah—yeah. No," he said, abruptly changing his mind mid-thought. "I shouldn't linger."

Then, without missing a beat, "Where's the panel box?" He was already halfway down the hall before Evelyn could answer.

"I … think it's in the pantry?" she offered, setting the box on the entry table.

Ernest popped his head back into the sitting room. "If it's in the pantry, that's criminal. Who hides a breaker box next to dry goods? That's how you end up electrocuting yourself reaching for a bag of sugar."

He turned a corner, muttering something about outdated codes, and Evelyn followed after him, half amused, half bewildered.

Ernest opened the pantry door and gave a low whistle. "Yep. There it is. Rusted shut like a treasure chest." He paused, crouched, and squinted at a spiderweb in the corner. "That's not even a house spider. That's a barn spider. I wonder how it got in here.…"

He reached up and gently knocked the web down with the back of a pencil he pulled from his shirt pocket. Then, without missing a beat, he said, "You have knob-and-tube wiring. I'm guessing this place hasn't been rewired since the early fifties, at best."

"Is that … bad?"

"Depends. Do you enjoy fire?" He grinned then opened the box with a pocket screwdriver and leaned in. "Okay, whoever wired this didn't trust the circuit labels, so they scratched in their own. In cursive. Why?"

Evelyn leaned against the doorframe. "You okay over there?"

"Oh, yeah. I love this stuff. I mean, it's a disaster, but it's my kind of disaster."

He closed the panel carefully—three times, in fact, pressing on each side to make sure it was flush—and stood up, brushing off his jeans. "Plumbing next?"

"Sure," she said with a smirk.

He zig-zagged through the kitchen, opened a cabinet under the sink, and immediately started pulling things out—old jars, rusted canisters, a glass ashtray shaped like a swan.

"These need to go. Sorry, but I can't think with clutter." He stacked the items neatly on the counter before sticking his head inside the cabinet. "Copper piping. Good. But you've got mineral buildup on the joints. That probably means low water pressure."

"I did notice the faucet stutters when I turn it on," she offered.

"Yup. I'd descale it, maybe install a pressure regulator if it gets worse." He sat back on his heels then pointed at the swan ashtray. "Do you want that? Because it's absolutely cursed."

She laughed. "Please feel free to throw it away."

"Thank you. That'll help me sleep at night."

Ernest stood, brushing the dust from his knees, then pulled his pencil from behind his ear like a man preparing to defuse a bomb. From his shirt pocket, he retrieved a small, spiral-bound notebook—creased and smudged from years of service.

"Alright, let's see…" he murmured, flipping to a fresh page. "You'll need caulk, a new outlet cover for the front room, vinegar for the pipes, probably a GFCI outlet or two …" He paused, underlining something with quick precision. "… and you're going to need all new wiring. Start with 12-gauge throughout. This whole place is still running on what looks like a death wish."

Evelyn's eyes widened. "All new wiring?"

"Yup. If it were up to me, I'd just gut it and rewire from scratch. But hey, no pressure."

She laughed — though it was slightly nervous. "That sounds expensive."

"It is," he said without hesitation, then he jotted down a few more items. "But cheaper than a house fire."

He tore the page out, folded it neatly, and slipped it back into his shirt pocket. "I'll stop by Bruce's shop after my route. He can open a tab for you. Just tell him Ernest sent you and look slightly overwhelmed. That usually gets you the 'local sympathy' discount."

"Does Bruce open tabs to everyone?"

"No. Just the charming ones."

Ernest grabbed the cursed glass swan from the counter and turned it over in his hand like it might bite. "Alright, you evil little thing. Let's find you a new home."

He carried it out with him, giving Evelyn a quick tip of his cap at the door. "I'll check back tomorrow — maybe get your water pressure up to something less medieval."

"Thanks, Ernest."

"Anytime."

As he crossed the yard toward his truck, he detoured to the driveway and gently lowered the swan into the trash can with surprising care — like he didn't want to offend it … just in case.

Then he climbed into the mail truck and drove off, waving once as he rounded the corner.

Evelyn lingered in the doorway for a moment longer before turning back inside, the quiet of the house settling in again.

The paper crackled softly beneath her fingers as Evelyn

shifted her weight on the dusty floorboards. Late morning light slanted through the study window, casting warm beams across the carefully stacked documents spread out around her as she finished her sandwich.

Each page was a copy — Gregory's doing. She'd asked him to pull anything connected to Ichabod Crane, and he had clearly gone above and beyond. The files were arranged in chronological order, complete with color-coded annotation tabs, sticky notes scribbled in sharp, slanted handwriting, and the occasional paperclip holding multiple references together.

Gregory might not have been the chatty type, but when it came to Sleepy Hollow's history, he was as meticulous as he was obsessed.

Evelyn flipped past a land record dated 1792 then a probate ledger from the early 1800s. A lavender sticky note stuck to the corner read:

Possible Crane property reference? Needs cross-verification with original plats.

She smiled faintly. Gregory had clearly gotten into this.

At the center of it all was a genealogy chart — drawn with fine, deliberate pen strokes and marked with updates Gregory had likely added by hand. Evelyn leaned over it now, eyes scanning the crisscrossing lines until her finger came to rest on a familiar name.

Donald Crane.

Her great-grandfather.

It was the only name she recognized.

Family history had never been a big topic growing up. Her

mother rarely talked about it, and Evelyn had never pressed. But now, as her gaze traced the branches climbing upward — name after name faded by time — she found herself staring at one near the top.

Ichabod Crane.

It was one thing to hear stories, to joke about ghost tales and old legends. Another thing entirely to see it laid out in ink and history. Tangible. Official. Real.

She let out a slow breath, her pulse ticking faster.

So it was true.

The legend was family.

Setting the genealogy chart aside, Evelyn reached for a plain envelope nestled between two clipped census reports.

The moment her fingers brushed it, she stilled.

Unlike the rest of the papers — neatly photocopied, annotated, and filed — this envelope was old. Really old. The parchment was yellowed, the wax seal cracked but still bearing the faded impression of what looked like a county crest or legal stamp.

She turned it over slowly.

This … wasn't a copy.

It was the only original document in the entire box. Somehow, it must have gotten mixed in by mistake — slipped between the pages without Gregory noticing.

Carefully, she broke the rest of the brittle seal and eased the contents out.

Inside was a folded letter, its ink slightly smudged with age, and behind it, a second page — more structured, formatted like a legal filing. Maybe a deed. Or a court record.

She read through them once.

Then again.

Each pass tightened the knot in her stomach.

If she was interpreting this correctly, the formal document referenced a series of land transfers between families—shifting boundaries, inheritance loopholes, irregular signatures. And the letter accompanying it wasn't casual correspondence. It was something between a warning and a confession.

Names stood out to her. Names she'd seen on storefronts. On signs. Names still spoken like heritage in this town.

Evelyn sat back on her heels, heart knocking against her ribs.

This wasn't folklore. This wasn't just Crane history.

This was a cover-up.

She slid the papers carefully back into the envelope, hands trembling. Then she stood, grabbed her keys from the hall table, and headed for the door.

Some answers needed professional eyes.

And Gregory Fenn would absolutely want to see this.

Chapter 12
Threads of Deception

The scent of old paper hit Evelyn as she pulled open the door to the records department. She stepped inside, the familiar creak of the door echoing behind her. Gregory sat at his desk beneath the harsh hum of overhead fluorescents, hunched over a map that looked older than the courthouse itself. He didn't look up.

"I brought something," she said.

He glanced over his glasses, recognition flickering in his eyes. "More Crane papers?"

"Something different," she replied, crossing the room and sliding the envelope onto the counter. "But possibly connected."

He opened it without a word and began to read, his brow furrowing as he scanned the letter. When he turned to the second page, his eyes sharpened.

"Where did you get this?"

"From you," she said. "It was in the box you sent with

Ernest Knickerbocker."

Gregory shook his head slowly. "I didn't put this in that box. I've never laid eyes on it before."

Evelyn's brow creased. "You haven't?"

"Certainly not. And I wouldn't allow an original document to leave this office—not under any circumstance." His tone turned clipped, more insulted than angry. "I'm meticulous when it comes to organizing this archive. If that envelope was in your box, then it found its way there via someone else. I don't make mistakes like this."

Several moments passed in silence—just the turning of paper, the soft buzz of lights, and the faint click of his pen tapping the desk.

Finally, he looked up. "It's real. Old but legitimate. This notation here"—he tapped a faded scribble in the margin— "that's not a clerk's mark. That's a redaction signal. Someone tried to erase this."

Evelyn crossed her arms, uneasy. "So ... what does it mean?"

Gregory's voice was quiet, almost reverent. "It means that a few founding families of Sleepy Hollow may have stolen land from the Cranes. Possibly others, too. It's not just fraud—it's legacy theft."

He stood and moved to the copier, making precise adjustments before feeding the documents through.

"This is ... substantial," he said as the machine whirred. "I'll dig into the original plats and probate ledgers. Cross-reference these names." He paused, eyes narrowing slightly. "I want to see how deep this goes."

Evelyn took the copies he handed her, her fingers brushing the edge of the paper. "So I'm not imagining things?"

Gregory looked up, his expression unreadable — but focused. "You've found something someone wanted buried. And frankly..." His mouth twitched at the corner, not quite a smile. "I'm very interested in what it all means."

Evelyn stepped out of the courthouse, the heavy door thudding shut behind her. Warm sunlight met her face — sharp after the dim, cool archives. She blinked against it, the crisp edges of the photocopied pages crinkling in her grip.

She hadn't realized how tightly she was holding them until she reached the bottom of the stone steps and paused, loosening her fingers with a slow breath.

Legacy theft.

Gregory's words echoed in her mind. What kind of secrets had she stumbled into? Why had that document been hidden — and preserved?

She tucked the papers into her bag and started toward her car, her thoughts churning with questions and theories.

"Evelyn?"

She stopped mid-step and turned.

Peter was coming up the sidewalk, a cardboard box full of miscellaneous items under his arm.

"Hey," he said with an easy grin. "Was just heading to your place."

She blinked, thrown off by the sudden shift in momentum. "Oh? Oh — right. I almost forgot."

"I grabbed a few things from the list on your fridge." He nodded toward the box. "WD-40, caulk, razor blades, painter's tape ... the usual suspects."

"That's really sweet. You didn't have to do that."

He shrugged. "I know. I want to."

It was times like this that made it difficult for her to see Peter as the devil Silas painted him as.

She smiled. "Thank you. I really appreciate it."

"Of course! Besides," he added, shifting the box to one arm so he could open the passenger door of his car, "I've been dying to see what other strange things that house coughs up."

She laughed. "There's a cursed glass swan in the garbage if you want to dig it out."

Peter gave her a mock-horrified look. "You threw it away? Bold move."

"According to Ernest, it gave off bad vibes."

"Ernest? Knickerbocker? He was at your place?"

She nodded. "Yeah, he dropped off a parcel for me—and very quickly became my handyman."

Peter chuckled. "Ha. Sounds like him. I bet you didn't even see it coming."

"Not at all," she said with a grin.

"Yeah, this town's full of doers. 'See a need, fill a need' types. It's one of the reasons I'll never go back to city living."

As he stowed the box in the backseat, Evelyn found herself smiling.

If she wasn't careful, she just might be in danger of actually staying in Sleepy Hollow—

Or worse…

Falling for the small-town guy.

Peter opened the passenger door of his car and gestured. "Your carriage awaits, my lady."

Evelyn gave him a mock curtsy. "Chivalry points noted."

Peter smirked and closed the door behind her before rounding to the driver's side. He slid into the driver's seat, glancing her. "You know… there's something different about you today."

Evelyn shifted in her seat. "Lack of sleep and mediocre instant coffee will do that."

He chuckled softly, then reached over — slow, not presumptuous — and tucked a loose strand of hair behind her ear. His fingers grazed her cheek, warm and gentle.

"No," he said quietly. "Not that."

Her heart thrummed at his touch. Evelyn couldn't deny how much she liked the familiarity — how natural it felt, the way he was already so comfortable with her.

She turned her face toward the window, hiding the smile that crept in despite herself.

"Was that a smile? No — wait — don't tell me. Did I just make you blush?"

She scoffed under her breath.

He gave a low, satisfied laugh. "Maybe there's hope for us small-town guys after all."

She buckled her seatbelt and offered a crooked smile. "Don't let it go to your head."

As they pulled away from the courthouse, the quiet hum of

the engine and the faint sound of gravel under tires filled the space between them.

"You looked deep in thought when I spotted you," Peter said casually, glancing over. "Find anything interesting?"

Evelyn hesitated. The papers in her bag suddenly felt heavier.

"Yeah," she said. "The more I learn about Sleepy Hollow, the more I want to separate fact from fiction."

She kept her tone light, almost playful. "Gregory's been helping me dig into the Crane family history. Turns out I might've inherited more than just a crumbling house."

Peter chuckled. "That so? I always figured those old family trees were mostly moss and scandal."

She side-eyed him. "You'd be surprised how much you can dig up when no one wants you to."

A beat passed. He didn't respond right away.

"I imagine some of it's better off buried," he said, almost under his breath.

Evelyn frowned slightly, but before she could press, he turned into the wooded road that led toward the Crane property.

The trees arched overhead, dappling the path in warm, golden light. Birds chirped somewhere in the branches, a stark contrast to the quiet dread that still lingered in her gut from the courthouse.

Peter tapped his fingers against the steering wheel. "Mind if I ask something?"

"Depends."

"What made you come here? Really."

She studied him a second longer than she meant to.

"I got a letter. A key. And no good reason not to."

Peter hummed thoughtfully. "Most people don't just uproot their lives for a mystery inheritance."

"Maybe I'm not most people."

He glanced at her and grinned. "That, I'm starting to believe."

They pulled into the drive, the cottage peeking out from behind the trees like it was still deciding whether or not to welcome her.

Peter put the car in park but didn't move to get out. "You know, I wasn't going to say anything … but word gets around. This town has ears in its wallpaper."

Evelyn tensed. "Let me guess. Someone's been talking."

He nodded once. "You might be surprised how quickly Carla's office leaks. And the name that leaked? Shuddered a few window panes."

She exhaled slowly, her hand tightening around the strap of her bag.

Peter held up a hand. "Look, I'm not mad. I get it. But I figured you'd tell me eventually."

"I wanted to," she said quietly. "But I didn't come here for attention. And I didn't want to hurt anyone."

"So who are you really?"

A beat passed. Then—

"Evelyn Crane."

Peter didn't respond right away.

His hand froze on the door handle, and for just a moment, the warmth drained from his face. Not in anger—but in recognition. In fear.

She watched the shift ripple through him—something quiet and instinctive, like a warning bell ringing deep inside him.

"So it's true," he said, barely above a whisper. "You're a Crane."

"I didn't want anyone to know," she said quickly. "Not because I'm ashamed but because there are people from the city who would kill to find me."

Peter turned to face her again, the grin long gone now. Not hard or cold—just distant. Measured.

"What, like mob trouble?" he joked.

She nodded. "Yeah, actually. The Russo family. I'm a journalist from The Post, and I wrote something they didn't want published. Now they want me gone."

He ran a hand down his face then looked out the windshield toward the trees. "That's a heck of a secret to carry."

"I wasn't trying to lie to you," she said. "I was trying to stay alive."

His gaze lingered on the tree line. "No, I get that."

But his tone had changed—softer now, heavier. He wasn't angry. He was worried. About her. About something else. But what?

Peter finally turned back toward her, managing a small, lopsided smile. "It's just … the Crane name carries weight here. You being back? That's not just history. That's … something else."

"You're not mad?"

"No." He shook his head. "But I'd be lying if I said it doesn't spook me a little."

Evelyn gave a soft laugh. "You? Spooked?"

114

He chuckled once, but there was no joy in it. "You have no idea."

Chapter 13
The Fog Rolls In

The silence in the car stretched longer than Evelyn expected. Peter sat in the driver's seat, fingers drumming lightly against the steering wheel, his gaze fixed somewhere beyond the windshield.

Evelyn cleared her throat. "I didn't mean to keep it from you … my last name."

Peter gave a small nod but didn't look at her. "Right."

"I wasn't trying to lie. I just — I didn't know anyone in town. I wasn't sure how people would react."

Still, he said nothing.

Evelyn shifted in her seat. "If this changes how you see me, I understand. I didn't expect to be handed a legacy I knew nothing about."

Peter finally looked at her, his expression unreadable. "It's not that."

She waited for him to elaborate. He didn't.

"Maybe we should just ... pick things up tomorrow," she offered, forcing a small smile. "If you're feeling up to it."

He hesitated then gave a quiet, "Yeah. That might be best."

Without another word, Peter opened the door and stepped out. Evelyn followed, surprised when he walked to the back and pulled the box of supplies and broom from the trunk.

"You really don't have to—" she started.

Peter didn't meet her eyes. "It's fine. I'll just leave them inside for you."

They walked up the overgrown path together, gravel crunching underfoot. The air had cooled, touched by the evening hush of the nearby woods. Evelyn unlocked the door, pushing it open with a groan of old hinges.

"You've done a lot already," Peter said, stepping inside and setting the box gently on the kitchen table. "Looks better than when I last saw it."

"Watch the floorboards," she said, trying to keep the mood light. "Some of them bite."

He offered a half-smile. "I'll consider it part of the charm."

She watched him for a moment—how naturally he moved, how familiar he already felt in this space. And yet ... something about him had shifted. His usual ease had dulled to something quieter. More distant.

"So," he said, stepping toward the door. "I'll see you tomorrow?"

Evelyn nodded. "Tomorrow."

Peter paused at the threshold, hand on the frame. He looked like he wanted to say something else—but didn't.

Then he was gone.

Evelyn shut the door firmly behind her and turned the lock with a quiet click. Despite Peter's reassurances, she couldn't shake the feeling she'd upset him — and what unsettled her most was not knowing whether it was because she was a Crane ... or something else entirely.

The rest of the day passed in a blur of dust and determination. Evelyn worked until her muscles ached — sweeping every corner, scraping cobwebs from windowsills, hauling debris to the porch. She opened every shutter she could, letting sunlight bleed through the gloom like fresh air for the soul. The scent of rot and mildew slowly gave way to cedar, lemon cleaner, and effort.

By sundown, the house still looked like it belonged in a historical horror exhibit ... but it no longer felt abandoned. She'd claimed it in her own stubborn way.

The tub in the upstairs bathroom groaned as she twisted the rusted faucet handles. At first — nothing. Then: violence.

The pipes rattled inside the walls like something alive, thrashing to get out. Water sputtered in sharp bursts, hissing, coughing, clanking. The floorboards under her bare feet trembled with each jolt.

"Nope," she muttered, twisting the knobs off quickly. The sounds continued for a few moments — another groan, another metallic knock — before finally settling into silence.

She sighed, too tired to be startled. She grabbed a clean washcloth from her unpacked tote, ran it under the cold tap in the smaller downstairs powder room, and wiped the day's sweat and grime from her face and neck. The water stung at a cut on her knuckle, but it felt clean.

She leaned toward the mirror, inspecting herself. Good enough for tonight.

Upstairs, the rickety iron bed protested as she climbed in. She pressed her back against the curved headboard, pulled the quilt across her lap, and laid a small stack of copied documents on her thighs—pages Gregory had pulled from courthouse archives. Property records. Family registries. Handwritten surveys.

She read slowly, absently rubbing a sore spot in her shoulder. Names repeated—Van Tassel, Van Brunt, Crane. Overlapping histories bound by land, marriage … and something else. Something sinister but veiled.

The floor creaked.

She froze.

Not the random settling of old wood. This creak had weight. Rhythm. A step.

"Silas?"

She waited, breath caught.

Another creak—closer. Near the doorway.

She set the papers aside and slipped out of bed. Barefoot, careful, she moved through the chilled air. The floor was cold beneath her soles.

She peered down the hallway.

Nothing.

"Silas? Is that you?"

Another sound—behind her.

She turned sharply, heart pounding. Nothing but shadows

and scattered papers.

She reached for the light switch —

Then stopped.

The curtain in the corner was moving.

Not swaying gently. Not drawn by wind.

Moving.

Pushed outward, as if someone had just stepped behind it.

"Silas, I know you're here," she said, crossing the room. "Still brooding over last night?"

She yanked back the curtain.

Nothing. Just the wall.

"Whatever. Don't want to talk? Fine. But go haunt somewhere else — I'm busy."

Then — behind her — a voice, low and rough:

"Leave it alone, Evelyn."

She spun around, her back hitting the wall with a thud, breath caught in her throat.

He wasn't there.

"Jeez," she exhaled. "Don't do that."

She scanned the room, every nerve stretched taut. "If you've got something to say, say it to my face. Stop playing games."

"You wouldn't like that right now."

"I already don't like this," she snapped. "So go ahead — yell at me for trying to find something that might give you a sliver of peace."

The temperature dropped. Curtains stilled. Even the walls seemed to hold their breath.

A shiver rolled through her as her breath clouded in the air.

"So dramatic."

And then—he appeared. Right in front of her. Dark. Towering.

"You need to leave," he said. "You shouldn't be here."

Evelyn glowered. "Excuse me?"

"You stirred something the moment you arrived. It's growing. I can't fight it. Not with you here."

"I'm not leaving, Silas. I have nowhere else to go. People out there want me dead."

"There are fates far worse than death."

"So what—just die? That your solution?"

"No. You don't belong in this house," he growled, stepping closer. "You're not a Crane."

Fear sparked—but so did fury.

She squared her shoulders. "Actually, I do belong here."

His eyes narrowed. "This place doesn't belong to outsiders."

"I'm not an outsider." Her voice cut through the air. "I'm Evelyn Crane."

Everything in him stopped.

The change was instant. His posture faltered. His expression cracked.

"… That can't be." His voice was barely above a whisper. "You're a Crane? That's … impossible."

He stared like the world had tilted. Hands curling—not in rage but disbelief.

"How can this be?" he murmured. "I was his friend. His only friend." His voice softened, ragged with memory. Regret. Loss.

"Tell me what happened that night. After Ichabod faced the Horseman."

He didn't answer, but darkness began to gather around him.

"Why are you so angry? You don't get to be. I should be angry with you. But I'm not. I'm the one trying to help you."

The muscles in his neck and jaw twitched.

"No. I don't believe you," he snapped. "You can't be a Crane. I would've known. Ichabod never shut up until I bellowed at him to stop. You must be lying."

The overhead light flickered violently, casting wild shadows.

Evelyn flinched. The bulb buzzed — then steadied — then sputtered again.

The curtains surged inward, billowing like storm-tossed sails —

But the windows were closed.

The air was still.

A tremor pulsed through the floorboards.

She turned back to Silas.

His jaw was tight. His fists curled.

Not a trick.

Not imagination.

Power. Grief. Rage.

His features sharpened as he stepped toward her.

Evelyn lifted her chin. "Is this where I scream and run?"

"Only if you're as smart as I think you are."

This side of him — raw and overwhelming — was new. Her eyes darted to the bed, where Gregory's pages lay.

"The family tree," she said, voice urgent. "I have proof I'm related to Ichabod. I can show you."

He didn't speak — but he stopped.

A beat passed. Heavy. Electric.

The light buzzed again … then steadied. The curtains froze mid-sway.

Silas stood motionless, his expression unreadable.

"Show me."

Chapter 14
Tethered

E velyn walked to the bed, her bare feet thudding softly across the worn floorboards. Her hands swept across the quilt, and papers fluttered, scattering across the bed. "Where is it—come on, come on—" she muttered.

Pages slid beneath her fingers like they were trying to slip away—birth records, land deeds, census rolls. Nothing yet.

Behind her, the room seemed to pulse.

The overhead light flickered violently, stuttering between dim yellow and shadow. A sharp, high-pitched hum bled from the walls and ceiling, electric and wrong. The old wiring trembled with it, and Evelyn could swear she felt it skittering beneath her skin.

Her stomach twisted.

She could barely breathe, heart slamming against her ribs—but she held her spine straight, jaw clenched. It wasn't that she was afraid of Silas. She knew that he wouldn't really harm her.

But he would do what it took to make her leave if he thought it would keep her safe. She knew that about him because of all of the nights he watched over her while she slept. All of the times he had comforted her when she was having panic attacks.

She flipped another handful of pages—shaking fingers, dry mouth—and then: there.

A heavier sheet. Curled at the edges.

"Here!" she gasped.

She stood too fast, bumping the bed frame with her knees as she turned. The family tree trembled in her grip.

"Here—Donald Crane. He was my great-grandfather." She jabbed a finger at the inked name. "This came from the town archive. Look at the line—that's my family."

The space between them felt electrically charged.

He stepped forward, boots whispering over wood. His eyes skimmed the parchment, but the muscle in his jaw twitched.

"Your name isn't on it."

Her breath snagged. "What?"

"You say you're a Crane. But this?" He glanced at the paper again. "This could be anyone's story."

Evelyn's pulse spiked.

She spun and lunged for her purse, yanking it open and tearing through the chaos inside—tissues, receipts, lip balm, pen—until her hand closed around her wallet.

She flipped it open and pulled out her driver's license.

"There. Evelyn Crane. That's my name."

She held it out like a shield.

He stared at the card. Something flickered in his expression.

Recognition? Doubt? He didn't move. Didn't vanish. But he looked at her — really looked — like the earth had shifted under his feet for the first time in a long while.

"Ichabod had a younger brother," she said, steadying her voice. "They were years apart. And from what I've heard … Ichabod was a little self-involved."

His eyes narrowed. "That fits," he muttered. Then quieter, almost thinking aloud: "All those others … the ones who kept coming here over the years. They were Cranes, too?"

"As far as I know," she said, tossing her card on the bed amongst the pile of papers.

A shadow passed over his face. Pain. Frustration.

"All these years," he said, voice raw. "All those opportunities — wasted."

"Opportunities for what?" Evelyn asked.

He stepped back, shoulders tightening.

"All this time … I could've been freed. From this curse. From this purgatory — "

"Tell me. Tell me about the curse."

Something cracked open behind his eyes. Desperation flickered there. Hope, barely formed and already retreating.

"Are there more Cranes?" he asked. "Anyone else in your family still alive?"

"I don't know," she said slowly. "I've never exactly been invited to a family reunion. As far as I'm aware, I'm the last."

His jaw clenched. He turned away, raking a hand through his blond curls.

"Of course," he muttered. "Of course. Fate finally sends

someone who could help me, and she's fifty generations too late."

"Help you how?" Evelyn asked, voice rising.

He turned back, and this time, his expression held longing. Weariness on the brittle edge of belief.

"Because only a Crane can break the curse that bound me here."

"Why would it have anything to do with my family?"

Silas didn't answer right away. His gaze shifted to the window, jaw tightening as if the memory physically pained him.

Then he spoke — low and bitter.

"It was platinum," he said. "Raw, unspoiled, and buried deep beneath the northern edge of the Crane property. Ichabod found it by accident — struck something strange while trying to clear the old creek bed."

Evelyn froze. "Oh my gosh."

Silas nodded once. "He didn't understand the full value of it, not then. But he knew it was rare. Knew it could change his fortune. That's when I told him — don't say a word. Not to Katrina, not to her father, no one. Wait until you speak to Knickerbocker."

"Bartholomew Knickerbocker," Evelyn whispered. "The legal clerk."

Silas's gaze slid back to her, surprised. "You know the name?"

She nodded slowly. "I saw it ... on an envelope. One I gave to Gregory to examine. It was old — seals still intact. I thought it might be a property filing or a letter that was never sent."

"It was meant for Bartholomew," Silas said. "Ichabod wrote it the night before the Van Tassel party. I helped him seal it myself. But he never delivered it. He got ... impatient."

"Because of Katrina."

Silas's mouth twitched with something too tired to be a smile. "He thought if he told Baltus about the platinum, he'd prove he could take care of her. Modestly, at least. He wanted a blessing. He got a death sentence."

Evelyn's stomach turned. She remembered the words from Ichabod's journal—"Everything's coming together. I just have to get him to listen."

She stepped toward Silas, holding his gaze. "They used the legend of the Horseman to get rid of him, didn't they?"

Silas didn't answer right away. His expression darkened.

"The Horseman didn't make an appearance on that road that night," he said. "Only a man wearing a legend like a mask. Ichabod trusted them. And it got him killed."

"And you were cursed … for trying to stop it." Evelyn's voice softened, the edge falling away. Each word landed slower now, steadier, as if she were finally beginning to see the full picture.

She looked at him—not as a ghost, not as a cautionary tale whispered in taverns—but as a man. One who had suffered for centuries not because he was a traitor but because he knew too much. Because they feared what he might reveal.

He'd tried to do the right thing.

And it had destroyed him.

Her throat tightened. She stepped forward slightly, gaze locked on his.

"You tried to protect him."

A pause.

"And they made it look like you ran. Left Ichabod on the road to face the Horseman alone. But they didn't curse you to punish you, did they?" Her voice dropped. "They cursed you to silence you."

Silas didn't reply. But something cracked in his expression — just for a breath. A flicker of pain. Of truth.

It was all the confirmation she needed.

Evelyn exhaled slowly, the ache in her chest blooming. She hadn't meant to care about him — not like this. But it was there.

Not pity. Not guilt. Something deeper. A pull she couldn't shake.

Her eyes locked with his, and her voice came low, unwavering.

"I'm going to help you. Whatever it takes. I mean that."

Silas didn't blink. Didn't speak.

His gaze had shifted — sharp but still. Like he was bracing for something he didn't believe he could have.

"You don't know what you're offering."

"I don't care." She took a step toward him. "You've carried this alone for too long."

His mouth moved, almost a smile — but it didn't make it.

"You've given me hope," he said. Then, quieter, "Even if nothing comes of it, ... I'll remember your kindness."

She hated how final that sounded.

He reached toward her — slowly, carefully — as though expecting the air to deny him or for her form to vanish at his touch.

But his fingers brushed her cheek.

A spark.

Heat shot through them like a current, alive and pulsing, as though something ancient was awakening.

Her breath caught.

Silas's eyes widened.

The sensation wasn't just physical — it was deep-seated. Like two pieces of the same thread finding their way back together after lifetimes apart.

Evelyn gasped.

It felt like the first breath after drowning. Like gravity shifting toward him.

Silas stilled, his eyes wide, lips parting — but not in fear. In awe.

Drawn to him, Evelyn lifted her hand and pressed it to his chest, her fingers curling into the fabric of his coat. She felt his heartbeat. Faint, distant … but there. Her throat tightened.

Something euphoric had stirred beneath the surface of their skin. Like their souls had been quietly stitched together long before either of them knew to look. Not a flare but a pulse. Steady. Low. Undeniable.

A bond.

Silas flinched.

Not away.

Toward.

Cupping her face in his hands. His gaze stayed locked to hers, something fierce flashing behind them.

"What is this?" he asked.

Her voice trembled. "I don't know. But I feel it too."

He gently took her hand from his chest and brought it slowly to his cheek, closing his eyes as he leaned into her touch like a man who had been starved of warmth for lifetimes.

"It has been centuries," he whispered, voice raw with wonder, "since I've felt another's touch on my skin."

Evelyn felt herself spiraling as they touched. Everything in her wanted to burst. She couldn't describe exactly what she was feeling, but it was deep and profound. A feeling so complex the only thought she could pull from it was home.

There was longing in his eyes, yes — but beneath it, something deeper. Fierce. Unshakable.

A collision of passion and devotion that made her breath catch.

Their bodies drew closer — not forced, not intentional, just inevitable.

The pull between them was now impossible to ignore.

His head lowered. Her lips parted.

She tilted toward him, every inch of her alive with the want of it, the rightness.

And still, beneath all of it, was the ache.

Because no matter how sacred this moment felt … they were still tethered to two different worlds.

Divided by death and breath.

Two hearts beating across a line that had never been meant to be crossed.

Yet here they were — touching.

Defying reason.

And daring the universe to stop them.

The room was still. Too still.

As if the house itself was waiting. Watching. Holding its breath.

Silas's hands framed her face, warm and steady, and she couldn't look away from him.

There was something in his eyes now — a rawness, a reverence — like she wasn't just someone who had touched him but someone who had woken him.

Her fingers slid along his cheek, slow and certain, memorizing the sharp angle of his jaw, the warmth of skin that should've been cold.

He wasn't a ghost anymore.

She didn't know what he was—but whatever he was becoming, she was part of it.

He leaned in—forehead brushing hers, light and hesitant. That small point of contact was enough to tilt the whole world.

Her chest ached. Her skin buzzed. Her soul reached for him.

"Evelyn," he whispered, low and reverent, as if asking for her permission to continue.

Her hands moved softly around his neck—opening herself up to accept him. "It's okay."

Keeping one hand on her face, Silas pressed the other against her back—his eyes moving across her face like she was something sacred.

Their lips hovered—so close—and she knew this wasn't just a kiss.

It was *the* kiss.

The one every poem tried to describe. The one every legend burned for.

She closed the distance.

And the world split open.

Light burst behind her eyes, pouring from somewhere deep inside her.

It wasn't gentle—it was powerful. Wild. Like something ancient had been waiting for this moment and was finally free.

The house groaned. The air shuddered.

Evelyn felt herself unravel — bone, breath, soul — everything falling into him.

Silas kissed her like he'd been waiting lifetimes.

Not careful. Not cautious.

Certain.

And she kissed him back with everything she had left.

The pull between them surged — hot and whole and right.

She felt the tether snap.

Not break — release.

The curse didn't scream. It didn't crack.

It just ... let go.

The space around them seemed to bend inward, hushed and electric, as if the air itself was holding its breath.

A faint shimmer gathered at their joined hands. Not bright, not warm — just a soft, spectral glow, like the breath of a candle behind glass.

Silver, threaded with pale violet, began to rise — curling delicately up her wrist, winding across his palm, illuminating the edges of their touch.

It wasn't fire. It wasn't flame.

The light didn't burn. It recognized.

It wrapped around them with the quiet certainty of something that had always been true. Fated. Claimed. Known. Not inked into skin. Not carved into flesh. But etched in memory. In magic. In something that existed beyond life.

Evelyn felt it sink into her — not as heat but as knowing. A wordless acknowledgment that their souls were no longer two separate beings.

Silas felt it too. She could see it in the way he looked at her — stunned, reverent.

Like he was witnessing a miracle he hadn't dared to hope for.

Then Silas stiffened again — his eyes lifting toward the window, cold and alert.

"What is it?" she asked.

He didn't answer at first, and the silence stretched too long. "Silas?"

His jaw flexed. "Are you expecting anyone?"

Her pulse quickened. "No. Why?"

Silas stepped toward the window, every movement slow and deliberate. "Someone's on the property."

Evelyn crossed to the other side of the room, peeking through the edge of the curtain. Outside, the fog had thickened again — so dense she could barely see the gravel path beyond the porch. But then she heard it.

Footsteps.

Heavy. Slow. Approaching.

"Is it someone from town?" Her voice barely carried.

"No." His voice was tight now. "Not someone friendly."

The floorboards creaked beneath Evelyn's feet as she backed away from the window. Her heart raced, but she forced herself to stay calm.

"What do I do?" she whispered.

Silas turned toward her, the tension in his face unlike anything she'd seen before.

"Hide," he said. "Now."

Evelyn rushed to the wardrobe, flinging it open and ducking inside. The wooden hangers rattled as she pushed through the few coats and long-forgotten dresses left by previous owners. Dust tickled her throat, but she pressed her lips shut, burying herself behind the hanging fabric. The door creaked as she pulled it mostly shut, leaving only the faintest sliver to see through.

Her heart pounded against her ribs. Too loud. Too fast. It felt like a beacon.

The footsteps grew louder.

Slow. Heavy. Measured.

They crossed the threshold of the house like a predator entering its den.

Then came the slam—a door downstairs, thrown hard against the wall. Another crash followed—something wooden splintering. A chair? A table?

Evelyn flinched with each blow.

"Come out, come out, wherever you are … ghosty."

The voice was deep. Gravelly. Wrong. It didn't sound like anyone she knew.

The voice sounded hollow. Twisted.

"You don't scare me," he drawled. "You never did. Hiding behind walls and rattling windows? Pathetic."

Another door slammed. A mirror shattered.

Downstairs, the chaos escalated—drawers ripped from their tracks, picture frames knocked from the walls.

Then silence.

Evelyn held her breath.

A whisper of movement—the stairs.

Each footstep up the staircase landed like a countdown. Ten … nine … eight …

Chapter 15
The Breaking Point

The wardrobe door flew open. Evelyn barely had time to react before Peter's hand shot in, grabbed her by the arm, and ripped her out with terrifying force. She hit the bedroom floor hard—ribs hitting the floorboards with great force, shoulder slamming into the corner of the bed frame.

The impact knocked the breath from her lungs. Peter towered over her, ax in hand, his eyes wild and sharp with something far older than anger.

"You know, I was really starting to fall for you. Trying to think of ways I could make things work for us."

His eyes were crazed as he spoke.

"Why did you have to poke your nose where it didn't belong?" he growled. "You and I could have been happy. A Crane and a Van Tassel. We would have been a powerful force."

"I could never be with someone like you." She spat the words like venom then kicked him in the groin before scrambling on her hands and knees.

Peter grunted, doubling over in pain.

Her heart hammered, and her vision blurred as she crawled. Her hand slid through broken glass from the shattered lamp— blood bloomed in her palm, but she barely felt it.

Peter lunged at her and dragged her back through the glass.

Evelyn screamed in pain, tears welling up in her eyes.

An electrical bolt from the light above struck Peter in the shoulder, and he fell to his knees. The windows blew open, and a terrible wind filled the space.

Evelyn rolled onto her knees and stood, stumbling out of the room. She made it to the hallway and was leaning on the railing, relying on it as she walked, when she was shoved to the floor. She dropped out of the way just before Peter's ax came down onto the railing where she had been standing. The ax easily ripped through the wood.

Peter stood, staring down at her as she slid backward down the hall, not daring to take her eyes off of him.

"Peter, you wouldn't go to jail for anything your family did. It wasn't you. You can still walk away."

"I would lose my home. Everything my family worked so hard to build would be gone. Nothing would be left." He raised his ax again.

"Please," she pleaded. "You don't have to do this."

"Oh, but I do. Or should I say, the Headless Horseman does."

"A ghost story would never hold up. You'll have to do better than that."

"Then I guess I'll have to suggest that the Russo crime

family was too cunning to lose track of you outside the city," he suggested. "Poor Evelyn. I couldn't save her. I tried so hard!" The ax came down hard.

"Ahh!" she screamed, rolling just in time.

The ax slammed into the floorboards, splitting the wood inches from her side with a sickening thunk.

Before Peter could rip it free, the house shook with a voice not of this world —

"Don't you touch her!"

Silas.

The warning wasn't just sound — it was force. It rattled the glass, vibrated the walls, made the air itself snap with fury.

A split-second later, the hallway mirror exploded.

Shards of glass shot like daggers, slicing across Peter's forearm as he raised his arm to shield his face. He cursed, staggering back, blood gleaming in streaks down his sleeve.

The air crackled — hot, electric, provoked.

The lightbulb overhead burst, sparks raining down like fireflies as darkness swallowed the hallway. The walls shuddered. The floor groaned. A pressure pulsed outward, like the house itself had come alive.

Silas was everywhere.

Peter growled, teeth bared, and spat into the chaos,

"Is that all you've got? You can rattle the walls, ghost, but it won't save her."

The house fell still.

But the stillness wasn't empty — it was charged.

The air pressed inward. Heavier. Denser.

The floor beneath Peter's boots gave a soft groan, as if something beneath the wood was waking up.

Then Silas's voice rolled through the space—not how it had before, distant and cold.

Now it came closer. Stronger. Grounded.

"You don't know what you've done."

Peter's smirk faltered.

The wind died. But the pressure didn't.

Instead, the shadows began to draw inward, like the house itself was folding around one presence.

A lamp shattered without warning. The ceiling cracked. The floor vibrated, just enough to make Peter shift his stance.

He looked around, unsettled now. Not afraid—but not laughing anymore.

"You're getting stronger," he muttered. A trace of unease in his voice. "But it's not enough to save her."

Evelyn crawled down the hallway, clutching a doorframe to pull herself up. Her legs shook, and her ribs ached—but she moved.

A bookshelf flew off the wall and crashed into Peter's side. He staggered, howling, but he didn't fall. Didn't stop. He came after her again.

Evelyn turned and kicked him square in the stomach.

He reeled back, just far enough she had time to reach the top of the stairs. Her bare feet slapped against the boards as she found her way down each one.

His heavy footfalls charged toward her, but it was too dark for her to move confidently.

She turned, desperate to see how close he was, but Peter grabbed her by the back of the shirt and yanked her off her feet. She hit the stairs hard — ribs cracking against the steps and her elbow denting the wall beside them.

She screamed. "Silas!" she choked.

Every light in the house exploded. But it didn't stop Peter.

He pulled her up into his arms and draped her over his shoulder like a rag doll.

"No one is coming to save you, Evelyn. Especially a three hundred-year-old ghost."

The house rumbled, its old bones groaning beneath Peter's feet as he carried Evelyn down the stairs like a sack of weightless defiance.

She kicked weakly — pain streaking from her head to her knees — but his grip was iron.

"Do your worst, Silas!" Peter barked, laughing darkly. "Nothing you do will stop me!"

The moment they reached the bottom step, the floorboards vibrated beneath them. Paint cracked along the walls. Lights above them flared and popped.

But Peter didn't stop.

He carried her across the entry, boots crunching over broken glass, and stalked toward the kitchen. With a grunt, he let her drop to the floor.

Evelyn hit hard — air knocked from her lungs — but she turned, bloodied hand reaching to pull herself back.

Peter lifted the cellar door beside her and shoved her closer.

"This is your last stop, Evelyn Crane."

The axe rose.

"Your final resting place."

Then—the house screamed.

Wind tore through the halls like a banshee—ripping open every window and door in a frenzy of force. They slammed open—then shut—then open again, the sound deafening. Curtains twisted like specters, wood groaned, and the ceiling above them cracked like it might cave.

Peter shielded his eyes from the swirling dust and chaos.

Evelyn didn't wait. She slid out from under him, dragging herself backward across the floor, heart pounding in her ears.

Peter roared, bringing the axe down toward her—and it stopped mid-swing.

Clutched in the hands of someone solid. Present. Furious.

Silas.

His fingers gripped the handle like iron, arm locked tight and unmoving.

Peter's face went white. "That's … impossible."

Silas's jaw was set, eyes glowing with a cold that didn't belong to the living—but wasn't death either.

Without a word, he yanked the axe from Peter's grip and hurled it across the room. The weapon slammed into the far wall with a thunderous crack, splintering the wood and sticking deep.

Then—it happened.

A low groan echoed from the house's very bones.

Silas faltered, breath catching. His body jerked, shoulders pulled back—like something was tearing him in two.

One hand clutched the air — life, golden and glowing, threading through his veins.

The other crackled with raw power — death, dark and electric, sparking across his skin like lightning wrapped in shadow.

Evelyn watched, frozen.

Silas didn't cry out. He grit his teeth, arms spreading wide as the energy between them pulsed harder, faster — fighting for him.

Then he moved.

He dragged both arms inward — clenching them to his chest like pulling the two realms into one body.

Power coiled around him, wrapping his limbs like cords of lightning and light. The glow of life met the fury of death.

And then — everything exploded.

The house shuddered as a wave of pure force imploded outward.

Sparks burst from the outlets. Plaster cracked from the walls.

The lights blew out — one by one — until darkness swallowed the room.

Evelyn cried out, shielding her face as debris scattered.

Silence followed.

Thick. Heavy. Final.

Chapter 16
The Reckoning

Smoke and dust hung in the air like fog. Ash fell from the ceiling like snow.

Evelyn's breath hitched.

"Silas?" she whispered.

No answer.

Peter groaned across the room and pushed himself upright, coughing. His confidence was already returning, a twisted grin tugging at his lips.

He took a step forward.

And then—the dust parted.

Kneeling in the center of the destruction … was Silas.

Head bowed. Shoulders rising with breath.

Alive. Whole.

And angry as hell.

He stood slowly, the floor creaking beneath his weight—not a ghost.

Not a whisper of who he used to be.

A force made flesh.

The glow in his eyes didn't fade. It deepened. And when he raised his head to meet Peter's gaze …

Death flinched.

Silas stood tall — unchained, unyielding. The shadows clung to him like armor. The air shifted with his breath.

The house — its bones old and haunted — seemed to brace itself beneath him.

Peter staggered backward, one hand reaching for the wall like it might steady him.

But Silas advanced.

Each step thundered.

The lights flickered in rhythm with his steps. Dust rose in his wake.

"You come from a line of cowards," Silas growled. "Murderers who hid behind myths. Who used a ghost to silence the only man who could have stopped them."

His hand clenched at his side, light and shadow flaring along his knuckles.

"For three hundred years, I rotted in your family's lie. Watching. Waiting. Powerless while you fed your legacy on blood and fear."

He stepped closer. Peter tried to back away toward the front door — but the house groaned and shut the door behind him.

Silas didn't slow.

"You people cursed me," Silas snarled, his voice trembling with centuries of fury. "Tied me to this land. To this town. And why?"

His eyes blazed.

"Because I told the truth."

"Everything my family did was to save this town," Peter shouted back. "It's because of us that Sleepy Hollow still exists. We made sacrifices you'll never understand," he spat, bitterness curling off every word.

"Sacrifice?" Silas roared, the sound like thunder cracking through stone. "You mean murder. You mean theft. And never at a cost that meant anything to you."

The wind coiled tighter around him now — wild, electric — like it, too, was hungry for vengeance.

"And now you want to bury her." His voice dropped to a low, deadly rasp. "Just like Ichabod."

He stepped forward, eyes cold and seething. "Allow me to show you what true death feels like."

Silas' hand shot out — his fingers gripping Peter's neck and pressing his body against the door. Waves of electricity danced across Silas' body, and darkness became his shroud.

Peter gagged and choked, doing everything he could to break free from Silas's hold — but it was no use. Silas's grip was unrelenting, his strength no longer just mortal.

"I warned you," Silas growled, voice low and lethal. "You shouldn't have touched her."

Peter's face turned a deeper shade, veins straining at his temples.

"Silas."

The word came quiet.

Evelyn.

Her voice cut through the storm like light through fog.

Soft. Certain.

She stepped beside him, hand finding his waist, the other gently wrapping around his outstretched arm.

"Don't," she said. "You're better than him."

Silas didn't move. But his jaw clenched, the fury still burning hot behind his eyes.

"He tried to kill you," he whispered, as if the words tasted like ash. "He would've buried you next to Ichabod without a second thought."

"I know," she said, voice trembling. "But we don't have to become what they are."

He looked down at her, breath ragged, the glint in his eyes shifting — pain, yes, but also trust.

"We have the evidence," Evelyn said, her grip tightening just slightly. "Everything we need to make this right. The letter. The deed. The names. Let the truth bury him, Silas."

Silas stared at her for a long, loaded second.

Then … slowly … he loosened his grip.

Peter crumpled to the floor, gasping, coughing — eyes wide with disbelief, like he couldn't fathom that he was still alive.

But Silas didn't look at him.

He looked at Evelyn.

His chest still heaved from the storm that had passed through him — but in his eyes, something quieter burned. Steady. Certain.

"I don't think I could ever defy you," he said, his voice low, the edge of battle still clinging to it. "Nor could I deny you anything. Not now. Not ever."

He took her hand and pressed it against his chest, the steady beat of his heart beneath her palm grounding her.

"I'm yours, Evelyn Crane. For as long as I draw breath. Maybe even longer than that."

Their foreheads touched. His lips hovered above hers—a breath away from sealing the moment.

But from the corner of her vision, she saw Peter stir, trying to crawl away, desperate to escape.

Silas didn't hesitate. His foot slammed down hard on Peter's back, pinning him like a tempest finally chained. Fire burned in his eyes.

Peter groaned, a sharp sound of pain and defeat.

Evelyn's breath caught—not from fear but a fierce protectiveness that blazed hotter than the pain lancing through her ribs.

"Don't," she whispered fiercely, eyes locked on Silas's. "You're finally free. Don't let him drag you back into that darkness."

Silas's gaze softened, haunted shadows flickering beneath the fire. "I won't," he vowed. "Not as long as you're here to keep me obedient. I don't think I could survive being alone again, but I would shatter into oblivion if you weren't here with me." His eyes shifted back to their natural dark blue.

Her fingers curled into his shirt, clutching like a lifeline. "You don't have to be the monster they made you. You don't have to be the curse."

He leaned in, lips brushing hers in a ghost of a kiss—tender, aching, full of promises.

"Then let me keep you," he said, bringing her fingers to his lips and pressing them softly there. "Say you'll stay."

She swallowed the ache in her chest, voice barely a breath. "I'm not going anywhere. I don't think my heart would allow it."

Silas lifted her effortlessly, holding her as if she were the most fragile thing in the world.

Outside, thick fog had rolled in, swallowing the world whole. It clung to the trees and crept along the ground like the breath of something ancient—just as the legends said, whenever the Headless Horseman was near.

The night air bit sharp against their skin as Silas stepped onto the porch. Red and blue lights pierced the mist, flashing through the white haze. The wail of sirens cut through the silence, growing louder—closing in.

Suddenly, a patrol car screeched to a halt at the curb. Officer Downey jumped out, flashlight in hand, rushing toward them.

"Is everyone all right?" Downey called out, eyes scanning the house and the fog.

Silas straightened, his grip protective but calm. "We're fine—just some bumps and bruises."

He turned, voice low but firm. "Peter Van Tassel is still inside the house."

Downey narrowed his eyes, stepping closer. "Who are you?" he asked with suspicion. "I've never seen you around town."

Silas met his gaze evenly. "I'm Washington Silas Irving."

Downey snorted, raising a brow. "Sure, and I'm the Headless Horseman."

Before Silas could reply, a sharp, unnatural whinny shattered the stillness—shrill and full of fury.

Then came the sound.

Thud.

Thud.

Thud.

Hooves—heavy and merciless—slammed into the earth, rattling the porch beneath them. The vibration climbed Evelyn's spine, a low hum of dread that gripped her ribs and refused to let go.

The fog ahead twisted violently, as if something immense was tearing through it from within.

A shape emerged—massive, spectral, and wrong.

The Headless Horseman.

He rode straight through the veil of mist, smoke trailing behind him like a funeral shroud. His armor gleamed wet with rot, the bloodstained sword in his hand catching the strobing flashes of red and blue.

He had no face. No eyes.

Only the unmistakable presence of judgment.

Evelyn gasped, pressing herself tighter into Silas's chest.

The Horseman didn't flinch at their presence. Didn't slow.

The pounding hooves shifted direction, thundering across the porch with deafening force.

Toward Peter.

"No," Silas breathed, voice caught. "He's not here for us."

The Horseman passed within inches of them, the wind he carried knocking Officer Downey off balance and stealing the breath from Evelyn's lungs.

The horse reared to a halt, and the Horseman dismounted in

one fluid, brutal motion — knapsack in hand.

His heavy bootfalls echoed through the fog as he stalked up the steps and vanished inside the house.

A beat later — Peter screamed.

It was short.

Followed by silence.

Then … the sickening sound of something soft and wet hitting the floor.

If Evelyn could have pressed herself any closer to Silas, she would have — but she was already swallowed in the safety of his arms.

The Horseman emerged once more, slower now. In his gloved hand, he gripped the knapsack — bulging, soaked through with crimson.

He mounted his horse as it pawed at the ground, nostrils flaring, eyes wild with the madness of the hunt.

As he passed them again, the Horseman jerked the beast to a sudden stop and turned his headless form just slightly — toward Silas.

Silas gently set Evelyn on her feet and stepped forward. Tall. Unafraid. Power radiating from him, no longer flickering but fully formed. A silent warning in his eyes.

The Horseman didn't challenge.

Instead, he dipped forward — a grim nod. Then tapped the bloodied sack now tied to his saddle. A silent contract fulfilled.

Silas gave a slow nod in return.

And then the Horseman was gone — vanishing into the fog as quickly as he'd come.

Silas exhaled.

The curse was broken.

And the price had been paid.

Evelyn sighed with relief and leaned into Silas's side.

He wrapped an arm around her shoulders, his hand rubbing slow, steady circles — comforting, anchoring.

Officer Downey stood in stunned silence for a long beat before clearing his throat. "It's a pleasure to meet you, Mr. Irving," he said, stepping forward and offering a hand. "I'm Officer Downey."

Evelyn tried to laugh, then winced. "Mm," she groaned. "Ribs."

Silas smirked and reached out, shaking the officer's hand with a firm grip.

"Likewise," he said. "Heck of a first impression, though, right?"

"It'll be a tough one to beat," Downey agreed.

THE END

Reviews are crucial for independent authors because they help readers discover books they enjoy. Please consider leaving a review if you enjoyed this book. Just a line or two is all that's needed, and it would mean a lot.

You can support the author by leaving a review on Amazon, Goodreads, and BookBub.

Subscribe to C. N. Noble's newsletter and follow her on social media so you don't miss out on any upcoming news!

ECHOES
OF THE HOLLOW

Dear Reader,

Welcome to Echoes of the Hollow—a story born from my love of folklore, legacy, and the shadows that follow us when the past refuses to stay buried. I grew up fascinated by the legend of the Headless Horseman, and this book gave me the chance to reimagine that myth through a darker, more intimate lens.

This is a tale of fate and free will—of what we inherit and what we choose to carry. Evelyn Crane didn't ask for a haunted legacy, but she's exactly the kind of woman who rises to meet it. And Silas? He's the rare soul who defies every curse and law of the afterlife … just to protect her.

Though this book is closed-door in terms of romance, it's rich with emotional intimacy, longing, and tension. It's for readers who like their stories dark, their stakes high, and their heroes willing to burn the world for the one they love.

Thank you for stepping into the fog with me. I hope the Hollow lingers with you long after the final page.

With gratitude and ghosts,

C. N. Noble

About The Author

C. N. Noble spent over twenty years as a closet writer before bravely stepping out of her introverted comfort zone. She is happily married and enjoys spending time with family, reading, gaming, gardening, walking in the woods, and pretending to have a social life. She's a high-functioning introvert who hides from unexpected guests, except for the UPS guy, who brings her book swag.